A NEW LAND
BOOK TWO

John
David's
Legacy

A New Land Book Two
John David's Legacy
Copyright © 2021 Areulia Davis

Cover Design: Fresh Design

ISBN: 978-1-7365129-1-3

10 9 8 7 6 5 4 3 2 1
Printed in the United States

Priceless Publishing
Coral Springs, Fl

www.pricelesspublishing.co

DEDICATION

Hi, I'm back!

This is the sequel to **A NEW LAND** that was published in 2018.
I could not have done it without the encouragement of the following persons:

To my parents:
Albert Jones and Rosie Lee Warren-Jones

To my sisters:
Grace, Allean and Jacquelyn LaVern (deceased)

To all my nieces and nephews.

To my loving husband:
Tyler Davis Jr.

To my talented daughter and son:
Brittni Octavia Cullar and Marcus Cullar

To my delightful and funny grandson:
Marx Langston Cullar

To all my relatives far and near, and some special seniors:
Dwight and Grace Thomas
Carrie LeNoir
Rev. Dr. Maxine Washington

To the Pastor and members of the Douglas Park Baptist Church,
To the faculty and staff of Stone Scholastic Academy in Chicago, Illinois.

Finally:
To all individuals who suffered a loss due to the
COVID 19 PANDEMIC, I am praying for you.

TABLE OF CONTENTS

THIRTEEN

AFTER JOHN DAVID

Olivia didn't remember a lot about that day. The days following the announcement of John David's death caused May-Lynn to go into a deep depression. She wouldn't talk or eat, most days she spent lying in bed under a quilt. Olivia and John Jr. worried about their mother and would check in on her daily. Jacob informed them that she had suffered a great loss, and she needed time to grieve. Sometimes they would pass her room and find her curled on the floor crying and chanting. Olivia would stand outside the door trying to understand what her mother was saying, but she never could.

Olivia tried her best to remember the man who was her father, but she could only recall little things. She remembered him working in the fields from sunrise to sunset and dragging himself home every night, barely able to stand. She remembers that he was a tall man. So tall that she had to look up in order to see his face. He would always greet her with a kiss and a smile.

One-night Olivia woke up after having a bad dream. May-Lynn was up heating his dinner as she always did. That night, she was reheating some stew over the fire when she looked up and saw her husband. When her father came into the house, Olivia sat up in the bed to greet him.

"Hey baby how you doing?"
John David came over and kissed May-Lynn on the cheek.

"Baby it's hard working for Mr. Johnson,
I don't know how much mo I can take."

May-Lynn shook her head in agreement.
"We're gonna do better real soon."

Then he noticed Olivia sitting on the bed.
"Hey baby girl why is you still up?"

Olivia reached up to her father.
"I wanted to stay up and see you Daddy."

John David laughed and said,
"Ok now that you see me, what do you want?"

He went over to the bed picked Olivia up and sat her on his lap.
"Tell me a story Daddy, tell me a story."

John David would start out telling Olivia about how his grandma and mother were brought over from Africa many years ago. He spoke about how they were slaves and worked on the Johnson plantation. He also would tell Olivia that her ancestors had spirituals gifts of healing and sight and they used these gifts to survive as slaves. John David looked at Olivia sitting on his lap he placed his callused hand on her head.

"Daughter you have these gifts also, but you must learn how to use them wisely. If you misuse them, you can bring yourself or somebody great trouble."

Olivia looked at her father.
"Daddy I got gifts? How do I used them?
Does John Jr. have gifts too?"

John David looked at his daughter and laughed.

"Hold on baby girl one question at a time. Yes! You got gifts, but you won't see them until you get older. John Jr. have gifts, but his gifts are not as strong as yours, this means you gonna have to watch and take care of him. Do you understand?"

Olivia looked into her father's eyes and nodded. That was the last time she remembered talking to her father.

Jacob and Ma Ellen kept the children busy, by taking them to the park the corner grocery store and to church. Olivia learned a lot from Ma Ellen. She stayed under her skirt watching her as she cooked and cleaned. Olivia would ask Ma Ellen all sorts of questions. They would sit at the kitchen table and talk for hours about everything. One sunny afternoon, Olivia asked Ma Ellen about the day when her father died. May-Lynn was upstairs sleeping and John Jr. had gone to one of the street fairs with Jacob.

"Ma Ellen can I ask you something?"

"Sure, child what is it?"
Ma Ellen responded.

Olivia continued, *"What happened to me that day when we found out my daddy been killed? I remember hearing my mama screaming, then I looked up and it was like I wasn't in my body, when I came back to myself, I was on the ground. What happened to me?"*

Ma Ellen looked at Olivia and sat down at the table across from her.

"*Baby when the white man brought our people from Africa, they thought that they had stolen everything from us, but they didn't. So, what happen was when we came here, we brought our Gifts.*"

Olivia repeated the word.
"*Gifts, Ma Ellen I heard that word before. My daddy told me about some gifts that me and John Jr. had.*"

Ma Ellen looked around the room expecting to see someone, but no one was there. She and Olivia were alone. Ma Ellen spoke softly. "*What did your daddy tell you?*"

"*He said that me his mama and grand mama had the gifts of sight and healing. What does that mean and when can we use these gifts?*"

Ma Ellen continued to speak.

(3)

"*Well the gift of healing is used to work on people when they sick, and the gift of sight is to look into the future.*"

Olivia looked at Ma Ellen with wonder in her eyes.
"*How do we get the gift? Is it given to them in a box or a bag?*"

Ma Ellen looked at Olivia.

"Well most times gifts is passed down from generation to generation, and it's real strong in womenfolk. My daddy's mama had the gift so when it was passed down to my daddy, him being the only boy it wasn't that strong. As a little girl when I would stand close to somebody, I would get a warm feeling that took over my whole body. I have the gift of sight, but it's very weak. One time a cousin on my mama's side came to see me. When I opened the door for her, I could feel the heat coming from her body. I looked in her face, and I could see the face of my mama. She had come to give me bad news about my mama, but before she could open her mouth, I knew that my mama was dead. That cousin left my porch and I never saw her again."

Olivia stared at Ma Ellen and couldn't believe what she was hearing, and it made her afraid.

"But how do I know that I have the gift,
and if I do what gift do, I have?"

Ma Ellen looked at Olivia.

"Baby girl it's by trial and error. You don't know what you have until it's time to use it. I believed what happened to you when your daddy died is that what yo mama felt in her soul came out of her and went into you. You notice that she's weak, right?"

Olivia nodded.
"She's weak because she's sad."

"That's right, but when she heard about yo daddy her grief took her gift away and went into you."

Olivia looked at Ma Ellen.
"That don't make no sense. I'm young, but I'm smart and that just don't make no since."

Ma Ellen looked at Olivia.

It's not supposed to make sense it just is. We were stolen brought over to this county not knowing what was going to happen to us, but we didn't know how strong and gifted we was. That's how we survived all those years being slaves. They thought they took everything away from us; our customs, our language, and our food. Trying to make us all over again. They couldn't take our souls and what we were born with from the very beginning. Now we just getting used to this new land and new living. We ain't *gonna never go back home because home for a lot of us ain't Africa it's Mississippi."*

And on that note Ma Ellen went back to preparing dinner for the evening meal. Olivia looked at her in wonderment and left the room. She went upstairs where her mama had been sleeping. She stood in the door of the room and saw her mother curled up in a ball lying on the bed. She almost turned to go when she heard her mother call out to her.

"Olivia come here."

Olivia turned and walked into the room.
She went over to the bed and asked her mother.
"How did you know it was me when you're looking at the wall?"

May-Lynn responded.
"I felt your presence."

May-Lynn turned and sat up in the bed. As Olivia looked at her, she noticed that her mother looked different. The hair around her head was white. Her skin was very smooth, and her eyes had turned from dark brown to light brown. Olivia just stared. May-Lynn took her daughters hand.

"Come to me child I must tell you something. The day your daddy got killed I saw him. I saw him fall in the river. When he fell in, I fell in. I saw the blood streaming from his body. I tried to save him, but I couldn't. He wasn't supposed to be saved; his time was up. I knew this but didn't want to believe it. I knew before we got on the train to Chicago, that we would never see him again, but I couldn't accept it. Now that he's gone a piece of me has died with him."

Olivia spoke.
"Mama why is your hair white?"

May-Lynn took Olivia by her hands and ignored her question.
"Baby when I first met your daddy, I was drawn to him, like a bee to a honeycomb. I didn't know him, but I did know him. I know it don't make sense, but the spirits had spoken to me and said we was supposed to be together. Some days we would sit in the woods and stare at each other. Our eyes spoke when our mouths didn't. One day before you and John Jr. was born, your daddy told me that his mama told him he was going to marry a girl named May-Lynn and have two children named Olivia and John Jr," May-Lynn said.

"Daddy's mama had the gift of sight huh mama?"
May-Lynn shook her head.

"That's how the spirit works child. Your daddy told me that the day he left his mama she was dying. He said he left the house where he was born and when he looked back it had disappeared like a puff of smoke. Olivia use your gift and use it wisely it can bring you joy, or it can bring you sadness. Whichever it is SIGHT OR HEALING you take control of it. You may have to use it to save your life."

May-Lynn laid down turned over and went to sleep. Olivia continued to look at her mother, then she remembered that she never answered her question.

FOURTEEN

MAY-LYNN'S FATE

For the next few months the family continued to live with Jacob and his wife. Slowly May-Lynn started coming around. She would come down to eat with her children and sit on the front porch. Many thoughts were swirling in May-Lynn's head. The one thought that wouldn't leave was that she and her children were now alone, and she didn't know how they were going to make it. Sometimes she wondered if it would be better for them to go back to Mississippi? That thought frighten May-Lynn because she hadn't kept up with her family, she didn't know if her parents were alive or dead.

One afternoon while sitting on the porch, May-Lynn looked out into the yard watching her children play. Olivia was chasing John Jr. around a tree. He would giggle when she caught him. They were so happy. She wanted to see them like this all the time, but she didn't know if she could make this happen.

The door opened, and Jacob came out on the porch.
Hi! May how you doin?"

May-Lynn looked up at him and smiled.

"Jacob I'm doin about as well as I can. Just knowing that I'll never see John David again makes my heart ache. I'm worried I may not be able to make a life for me and my family, we're all alone."

Jacob looked at her.

"What do you mean, you got me and Ma Ellen, we're your family now, and we'll take care of you. Have you heard anything from John David's brother?"

"I haven't seen his family, since they told me the news about John David. Plus, I don't think my sister-in-law likes me. I don't want to bother them if I don't have to."

Jacob spoke up.
"Girl we ain't gonna let you stay out here by yourself. I don't know about John's people, but we'll always be here for you. In a few days we'll sit down and decide what we gonna do next don't you worry."

May-Lynn looked up at Jacob.

"Thank you! Jacob, thank you so much.

The next few days May-Lynn took back her role as a mother. She would get up every morning and help with her children. She went to the store with Ma Ellen and even took her family to Jacob's and Ma Ellen's church on Sundays. One Sunday after service Ma Ellen invited the pastor and a few members back to her house for a big dinner. May-Lynn helped prepare Mac & Cheese, Collard Greens, Ham, Hot Water Corn Bread, Candied Sweet Potatoes, Black Eyed Peas, Peach Cobbler for dessert and Sweet Tea. While working in the kitchen May-Lynn brought up the subject of the day when she heard the news about John David.

"Ma Ellen!"

"Yes sweetie."

"You remember what happened when I got the news about John David don't you?

Ma Ellen stopped what she was doing and looked at May-Lynn, then she looked for a chair and sat down. She all of a sudden seemed very tired. May-Lynn sat down in a chair across from her.

Ma Ellen spoke.
"I wasn't there but Wilma told me the whole story. She told me how you fainted and fell to the floor. Then she told me about Olivia."

May-Lynn looked at her in surprise.

"What about Olivia? What happened to Olivia? Wilma said that before her husband told you about John David, she took the children to the backyard. Olivia heard you scream, then she screamed. Then Wilma said she watched as Olivia started rising from the ground and she just floated in the air. Then she fell back on the ground in a deep sleep. Wilma said when she woke up, she didn't remember anything."

May-Lynn sat back and looked at Ma Ellen. She couldn't believe what she was hearing, she thought that Olivia would receive the gift much later she was too young.

"What did Wilma say about John Jr. was he scared? Wilma said he just cried when he saw his sister floating, he ran to her when she fell and laid next to her on the ground. Did he ask any questions?"

"I don't remember."

Ma Ellen went back to fixing dinner.

May-Lynn stood and walked to the front of the house. The guests were standing around, waiting to be called to dinner. She stood on the porched and watched as Olivia played a game of checkers with Jacob. John Jr. stood by helping Jacob move the black checkers on the board.

Olivia looked up at her mother. She stared at May-Lynn looking as if she could see right through her. May-Lynn looked deep into Olivia's eyes all of a sudden, they were the only ones on the porch. Jacob and John Jr. had disappeared, and so did all the guest. Olivia stood in front of her mother; she was no longer a little girl she stood as tall as May-Lynn. Her face was more mature. She looked about the age of 15 or 16.

Olivia spoke to her mother.

"Mama don't worry about me and John Jr. we gonna be alright. I know you love daddy and want to be with him, it's ok! We love you mama!"

May-Lynn blinked a few times, when she opened her eyes, she saw Olivia smiling at her as she continued to play checkers with Jacob. She shook off the vision and told everyone that dinner would be ready soon.

(2)

May-Lynn continued to get stronger. She spent a lot of time with her children, playing with them and taking them on long walks. She ventured into the city, discovering new neighborhoods. She figured one day they would move, and she wanted to see what apartments were available in the area where Jacob and Ma Ellen lived.

One evening before dinner, Jacob was sitting on the porch, May-Lynn came and sat in the seat across from him and spoke.

"Jacob, I love you and Ma Ellen so much. You've been a Godsend since the day I stepped off the train. I thank you for your sincere love for me and my children, but I think it is time for us to go. I feel ready for us to start a new journey, "our journey", so if you can help me find a job and a place to live, we'll be moving soon."

Jacob looked at May-Lynn as if he was looking at his own daughter. He had grown to love her and her children as if they were his own. He didn't want them to leave, but he understood that it was time for them to find their own way.

"Now May-Lynn you know that you can stay here as long as you need to. But at the same time, I know you have to start a life for you and your children. They'll be going to school soon and ya'll want your own place to live. We will always be here for you. We're your family now, and even though John David's brother is here, I want you to remember that we love you and whatever you need, we're for you."

He stood and pulled her to her feet. May-Lynn stood and put her arms around Jacob. Hugging him so tight she didn't want to let him go. She hadn't felt this way since she had left her father. When they pulled away, they both had tears in their eyes. Ma Ellen stepped out on the porch and saw the two crying.

"What's going on out here?
What did you say Jacob to make May cry?"

May-Lynn started laughing and Jacob looked at his wife.

"How come I'm always the one in trouble?"

Ma Ellen replied.

"Because you always doing something."

May-Lynn jokingly said.

"Woman you know you get on my nerves."

Ma Ellen ready to serve the dinner she prepared says.

"I don't care about your nerves, you two better come in here and eat before my food gets cold."

Jacob gathered the two and led them into the house. That night at the dinner table Jacob prayed a special prayer.

"Dear Lord, tonight I'm asking for a special blessing. I am asking you to bless and embrace May-Lynn, Olivia, and John Jr. They will be leaving us soon and I'm asking that you keep your loving arms around them. Hold them tight, with your love. Your grace and mercy will keep them in this mean world and city. I am asking and begging you Lord to take care of his daughter and these beautiful

children. Bless this food which we are about to receive for the. begging you Lord to take care of this daughter and these beautiful children. Bless this food which we are about to receive for the nurturing of our bodies Amen."

Jacob looked at the group around the table everyone was silent. Olivia looked first at Jacob and then at her mother all of a sudden, the room became dark. Everyone disappeared and Olivia was alone sitting at the kitchen table. She saw a light coming from the ceiling. She glanced up and saw a figure dressed in white. As she looked closer, she could tell that it was a man. He came down and stood in front of her. As Olivia looked closer, she was trying to recognize the face. The man sat down in one of the chairs and called her name.

"Olivia, it's me daddy!"
Olivia gasped, stood suddenly knocking over the chair.

"Don't be afraid baby, I just come to check on ya'll I miss ya'll terribly That day in the woods, when we was going to the train, I felt in my soul that I would never see ya'll again and it came true."

Olivia continued to look at her father. He stood there, and appeared to be transparent. She literally could see right through him. A yellow light surrounded his body. His clothes were worn and dirty, and on one sleeve it appeared to be blood stains. Olivia started to speak but he spoke first.

"Baby girl I don't have long to talk to you, so I want you to listen to me carefully. I want to tell you about your GIFT. Back in Africa yo ouma (great, great grandmother) was the spirit doctor for our tribe. She had the gift of HEALING AND SIGHT. The gifts are passed down to the first girl. I was sent to tell you that you have the GIFT OF SIGHT but not the Gift of Healing. This means daughter that you can see into the future, but you can't heal or cure diseases."

John David's eyes became dark.

"Olivia because you don't have the gift of healing, you need to know that you won't be able to help the ones you love."

Olivia heard her father and whispered in a scared small voice.

"Daddy what do you mean I won't be able to help the ones I love? Daddy why are you here? Why did you come to see me and not mama? You're scaring me I don't believe that I am seeing you and I can hear you. Why did you come to see me?"

John David didn't answer her. John David looked at his daughter and spoke.

"I'm here to warn. Just because you have the gift does not keep you, John Jr. and your mother safe. You have to be careful at all times. Always look around you and beware of evil. Your gift is special, but it can be a threat to people."

"Daddy what about mama's gift? Can't she protect us?"

John David answered.

"Olivia your mama's gift is weak. We were strong in life but we're weak in death. You have to be the one responsible for your mama and brother. You can do it. I see the gift of sight in you and it's very strong. Use it wisely and it won't fail you."

Olivia wanted to ask more questions, but as she looked at her father he started to fade. A blue smoke started surrounding him and he got smaller and smaller. She called out to him, but he only waved a hand at her, then he disappeared.Olivia never did tell anyone about that day, especially her mother.

FIFTEEN

THE APARTMENT

Thatfall brought cold weather to the city of Chicago. May-Lynn decided it was time for her family to move. Jacob had helped May-Lynn find a job working as a maid for a family in the Lawndale neighborhood. May-Lynn thinking of her family's future, worked day and night saving money to rent an apartment. One day Jacob rushed in the house with the news that he had a friend who had a small two bedroom flat to rent. The good news it was not too far from their house.

On the day they left, May-Lynn and her children gathered the few belongings they owned and they stood on the porch with Jacob and his wife. They really hated to leave, but without John David it was important for them to start a life in Chicago. Ma Ellen had tears in her eyes, as she went around hugging each of them. John Jr. sat on the step with his head in his hands. He was especially sad because he didn't want to leave Jacob. Jacob sat down beside John Jr. and spoke to him.

"*Little man don't you be sad because I'm still gonna be around for you. You come by to see me whenever you want, you hear me?*"

Then he pulled John Jr. to him and gave him a hug.
John Jr. looked up at Jacob with tears in his eyes.
"*I'm gonna miss you Jacob, please don't forget me!*"

Ma Ellen spoke up.
"*I'm gonna miss ya! You know you're my family and if you ever need anything you just come and see me, you hear.*"

Ma Ellen waved good-by and ran into the house.

Jacob gathered the group and together they walked two blocks to a rundown tenement located on Western and Ogden. The apartment was located in the back of the building. They walked down a dark gangway to a side door. May-Lynn looked up. The building had decaying bricks and broken windows. Not what she wanted for her family but there were no other alternatives, this would have to do for now.

Jacob knocked on the door and called out.
"*Hey! James Jr. it's me Jacob.*"

Above them a man looked out of one of the broken windows and yelled out.

"Hi! Jacob I'm coming right down."

A wooden scared door was pulled open. A short dark man, with a beard stepped aside and motioned them to come in. He wore a plaid shirt and overalls. He smiled at them, showing a mouth with missing teeth.

"Come on in I'll show you the flat. It just became available. People moved out last week, of course you got to take it as is. Didn't get a chance to clean it. If I cleaned it that will be ten dollars extra."

May-Lynn spoke up.

"That's ok we can clean it ourselves."

The man man replied.

"Fine with me! Let's go upstairs it's on the second floor."

The group continued up a dark staircase. After landing on the second floor, they walked down a narrow hall with doors on either side. Noises and sounds filled the stale air, voices, music and babies screaming. James stopped in front of a door that stood partially open.

"This is the bathroom for the floor, you have to share it with four other families, so you better get up early to do your business."

May-Lynn looked at the bathroom in disgust. There were rags hanging on a line that stretched from wall to wall. Paper was on the floor and a strong stench hung in the air. James led the group to the last door at the end of the hall. He took out a pair of keys and handed them to May-Lynn.

(2)

May-Lynn opened the door to the two-bedroom apartment and looked around. The apartment was small and cold. The walls were a dirty white, with streaks of cobwebs stretching from wall to wall. On one side of the small living room, sat a brown sofa that was very low on the floor. Beside the sofa was an overstuffed dark-blue chair with cotton coming out of the cushion. The group continued through the apartment, they located a kitchen, a bathroom, and two bedrooms. In the kitchen there was a stove, and an icebox. The icebox door was slightly open. May-Lynn, looked Inside and found an old bottle of spoiled milk. She took it out and screwed up her nose. She walked over to the sink, and poured the liquid out, she turned on the faucet and watched as brown water sputtered into the soiled sink. She turned off the water and looked at Jacob. He looked at her and frowned.

"Now May-Lynn if this is not what you want, we can find something else. It's up to you!"

"No! It's going to be okay we can clean it up and put in some pretty pillows and flowers and we'll be just fine."

She pulled her children into her arms and started to pray. Jacob and James bowed their heads, also.

"Dear Lord, I thank you for giving me and my children a place to stay. We thank you Lord for keeping us safe. I thank you for Jacob and his wife Ma Ellen, they're our real family now and we appreciate and love them. Continue to bless them and keep them in our lives. This I pray in Jesus name, Amen."

And the group said *"Amen."*

May-Lynn looked at her children, covered her mouth, and started to cry. Olivia now almost as tall as her mom, put her arms around her mother and said.

"Mama don't cry I know it's hard to forget that Daddy is gone but we're going to be alright. You, me and John Jr.

The little family settled in their new surroundings. It wasn't the best accommodations, but they had a roof over their heads, and food to eat. May-Lynn, with the help of Jacob and Ma Ellen registered Olivia and John Jr. in Gladstone Elementary School. Olivia was in the second grade and John Jr. was in the first grade. The children hadn't attended school in the south, so they were behind the other students in the skills of reading, writing and math. They also had to get use to leaving their mother every day and going to a building filled with strangers.

John Jr. hated school immediately. He expressed this to his mother and sister. He was having a hard time with his studies. He would easily get frustrated when he couldn't remember the Alphabet or count. He would throw his pencil across the room when he couldn't write the letters to his name. He didn't get along with the other boys in his class. He was teased and taunted because he wouldn't talk. When the teacher asked him a question, he would put his head down on his

John Jr. had the soul of a loner, even at the age of 6. He could be found in a corner staring at nothing in particular. He also kept a lot of his thoughts to himself. May-Lynn and Olivia soon found out that the only person who John Jr. would talk to was Jacob. May-Lynn didn't like seeing her little boy sad. So, she made it her business to let John Jr. see Jacob at least once or twice a week if did his homework and his chores. John Jr. was satisfied with this arrangement.

Olivia on the other hand was very excited about school. She noticed that the students in her class were more advanced in their studies, so she asked for extra homework so that she could catch-up. Her favor subject was reading. She would go to the neighborhood Library and take out 3 to 4 books to read during the week. What Olivia enjoyed most was reading to her mother. She would ask her teacher if she could take her Sally, Dick and Jane book home to practice and her teacher would always give her permission. Olivia would sit in the kitchen while May-Lynn fixed dinner and read story after story until her mouth got dry. Olivia always wondered if the stories she read was real, they were always happy and joyful. May-Lynn was happy with Olivia's progress in school.

"Olivia I'm so happy that you're doing well in school. You know, Negros can do more things in life, instead of sharecropping, being a maid, or cleaning up after folk. Your daddy didn't go to school at all, and I only finished the 7th grade. We might have been a lot further if we'd gone to school. You keep studying so that you can have a better life than me and your daddy. Ok baby girl?"

Olivia said. *"I will mama."*

In spite of everything going on, May-Lynn's heart still ached for John David. She even saw him in her dreams. One night, she woke up in the middle of the night and saw John David standing at the foot of her bed. He looked like the young man she had met many years ago. She sat up and stared. She knew she was dreaming, she reached out to him hoping to touch him, but he moved away.

Hey! May, if you touch me, I'll disappear, (he smiled) Oh honey you don't know how much I want to touch you, hold you in my arms, I miss you and the children so much. I worry about you all the time. But I know that ya'll are gonna make it. I trust that you will raise my babies and take care of them. But May you have to take care of yo self too. Stop grieving for me, I'm gonna be alright, don't you worry bout me."

In the coming weeks, John David appeared to May-Lynn two more times, always delivering the same message. Somehow the message helped May-Lynn go from day to day, giving her the courage, to go on. One night, May-Lynn found herself not being able to sleep. As she laid in bed looking at the ceiling, she noticed a light the size of a quarter. She had never seen it before. She had the strange feeling this was not a natural light. She sat up in bed. Continuing to stare at the light it started to get bigger and bigger, so big that it completely filled her room. At the foot of her bed stood John David, and beside him, holding his hand was Olivia.

May-Lynn cried out:

"Oh, my lord what is happening? John David

why do you have Olivia? Is my baby dead like you?"

John David looked at May-Lynn and spoke.
"May-Lynn this is going to be my last visit to you,
Olivia is not dead. She's a part of this dream."

May-Lynn looked at her daughter and she could see
that her eyes were closed. She called out to her.
"Olivia, Olivia, wake up baby."

Olivia opened her eyes, but she appeared to be in a trance,
she spoke.
"Who called my name? Mama, Mama, is that you,
where are you I hear you but I can't see you."

Then Olivia looked and saw her father.
"Daddy you're back I thought I would never see you again.
Why are you here?"

"Baby I'm here to talk to you and your mama."
"Where's Mama?"

"She's here you can't see her, but don't worry she's ok. May-Lynn
call out to your daughter to let her know you're here."

May-Lynn was now shaking, this was totally different from the other dreams she'd had. She didn't know what John David was doing, but she trusted him, so she spoke.

"Olivia baby I'm here, I'm sitting on the bed."
"But mama how come I can't see you?"
"Let's just listen to your daddy, you'll be ok."

Olivia looked up at her father as she continued to hold his hand. John David looked at his wife and glanced down at his daughter.

"May-Lynn I'm not going to come to you no more, my job is done. I'm here to warn you and Olivia about the future. May it's not gonna be easy raising these children, but I know you gonna do your best. I trust you."

John David suddenly stopped talking, he let go of Olivia's hand and placed his hands on his head. John David lifted his eyes to the light coming from the ceiling in the room. He started to sway appearing as if he was going to fall. All of a sudden he yelled, ***"Be careful of…be careful of the house on 19th street. Don't go there. DANGER! There's danger inside the house. There's death inside the house!"***

May-Lynn looked at her husband in horror.

"John what are you saying? Why are you talking about death? You're scaring me, what are you talking about?"

John David stopped yelling and fell to the floor. May-Lynn jumped out of the bed and ran to her husband. Olivia was standing on the spot where her father left her. Her hands were raised above her head, her eyes had a yellow glow. May-Lynn called out to Olivia as she kneeled down beside John David. She tried to touch his body but there was something invisible covering him that would not let her touch him. May-Lynn continued to watch her husband as he laid there. All of a sudden, he was surrounded by a bright light that blinded May-Lynn. She was forced to close her eyes and when she opened them John David was gone. Olivia was standing near her mother not saying anything, there was a blank look in her eyes.

May-Lynn stood up and went to her daughter.

"Olivia, Olivia can you hear me? Baby are you alright?"

Olivia blinked her eyes and looked at her mother and spoke.

"Mama I'm alright, and we're going to be alright no matter what happens in the future."

She spoke in a matter of fact voice that made May-Lynn take notice. Olivia spoke in a mature voice that made Olivia seem older. Olivia spoke.

"Mama I know that you're tired, you go to bed and get some sleep."

Olivia went back to the room that she shared with her brother. He was still asleep and hadn't been disturbed by what had happened in her mother's room.

SIXTEEN

CHICAGO:
THE DEPRESSED YEARS

Chicago, IL in 1910

T he next 7 years were hard for May-Lynn and her children. Olivia was now 14 and John Jr. was 13. Chicago was a crowded *melting pot of culture*. Polish, Jews, Negros, Italians, and Spanish were just a few of the ethnic groups that had settled in Chicago. Negros, would come by the thousands, seeking a better life, but there were never enough jobs for everyone. Everyday there were long lines of men and boys standing outside of factories, waiting to get hired for the day. When the doors, opened in the morning, the foreman would announce how many jobs were available.

"I only got 10 jobs for the first 10 men."

As the men stood in line the foreman would step up to each man counting. "One, two, three, four, five, six......" Then he would notice a Negro standing in line and suddenly say.

"That's all for today. I forgot I only got six spots, sorry that's it everybody go home."

It wasn't fair but that's how it was, Negros started to realize that things were, not so good *"up North"*.

May-Lynn continued to work for a variety of families in the Lawndale Community. She was hired to cook, clean, and watch the children of the house. Most of the families were good to her as long as she stayed in her place. However, just like the South she was required to enter and leave through the back door.

When the families entertained, May-Lynn was required to wear a black and white uniform, which emphasized her position of being a maid. If the mother and father went out for the evening, they would request that she spend the night. She never did. May-Lynn would tell her employers, that she too had children and didn't want to leave them alone. She was quickly fired on the spot. They didn't respect May-Lynn or her life.

Sometimes while walking to work May-Lynn would admire the beautiful houses, with large picture windows, front porches, and beautiful green lawns. She wondered if she would ever be able to afford a house in the neighborhoods where she worked? She was finding out more and more, that living up North was not much different than living down South. Negros fought hard for housing and jobs. The city was sectioned off with invisible boundaries, silently telling Negro's where they could and could not live.

Even though there were many cultural groups in Chicago, Negros were still considered the least respected group. This caused the Negros in the city to build support groups to help each other. Many days there was not enough food in the house, but with the help of generous neighbors they never went hungry. Sharing dinner was a common occurrence in the Negro communities. Everyone was aware of the struggles families faced those days.

So it was natural for people to help each other, and it was called being *hospitable* - a tradition from the South. In the building where May-Lynn lived, neighbors would knock on apartment doors telling everyone to come and get a bowl of soup, greens, beans or stew. People would, line up in the hall with plates and bowls, men, women, and children. Sometimes someone would add "hot water cornbread" to the meal, then someone else would add sweet tea, a sweet potato pie or "teacakes". Before long one bowl of soup would turn into a five-course meal. Everyone would go to bed that night with full bellies.

Jacob and Ma Ellen stayed in touch May-Lynn and her family. They would have them over for dinner at least once a week. Jacob with concern in his voice, would ask how things were going. May-Lynn would answer with hesitation that things were "as well as they could be". Jacob could see that she was still not comfortable about living in Chicago. She stated that because she no longer had John David, she still needed that family connection. She wondered if members of her family were alive or dead. It made her sad that she had no way of contacting them. She expressed one day to Jacob.

"Jacob, I have dreams about my family. I haven't heard from anyone in years. Sometimes I think about going back down south just to check on them. I miss them so much."

She said with tears in her eyes. Jacob felt sorry for her. He didn't know how to comfort her. His Mississippi connections also had vanished. He heard that a lot of families had scattered throughout the South. Times were very dangerous with the segregation and lynching's taking place all throughout the South. May-Lynn reminded Jacob of a "fish out of water". He came to the conclusion that she would never fit in up North.

During their weekly visits, Ma Ellen would give Olivia and John Jr. clothes that had been donated to her church. Olivia was very grateful, but John Jr. would complain that he didn't want any hand-me-downs. May-Lynn would chastise her son who was becoming very difficult as he got older. John Jr. detested how they lived. He felt they should have more. Many days he would complain to his mother that she should let him work instead of going to school where he wasn't learning anything. May-Lynn refused to let him quit school.

John Jr. continued to grow close to Jacob. He could hardly wait to see him each week. They would sit on the porch in the evening waiting for Ma Ellen to call them in to dinner. John Jr. still didn't like school, and he would express his thoughts to Jacob. Jacob would tell John Jr. how important it was for him to stay in school. He emphasized that a Negro in America could only better himself by going to school.

The white man has always been afraid that if a Negro gained an education, he would know just as much as he does or maybe more. John Jr. still was not impressed. He felt he would be able to serve his family more if he worked. May-Lynn continued to say no to John Jr. working and Jacob didn't want to go against her. She was his mother and she had the last word. Ma Ellen kept a garden, and at the end of the summer, she would always share greens, tomatoes, potatoes and peppers with May-Lynn. She taught Olivia how to can fruit and vegetables for the winter. May-Lynn was very grateful, she knew she never would have made it without the help of Jacob and Ma Ellen.

One of the last days of summer, May-Lynn was sitting on the porch with Jacob. She had been vexed for the last few weeks worrying about her family.

"Jacob I'm thinking about going back to Mississippi for a visit. I don't want to take Olivia or John Jr. because it's almost time for them to go back to school. I was wondering if they could stay with you and Ma Ellen for a while until I come back?"

Jacob looked at May-Lynn expectedly, knowing that this had been on her mind for a long time. He answered her slowly.

"May-Lynn are you sure you want to go back.
Why are you going back?"

May-Lynn looked at him and sighed.

"I need to know if I still have family back home, and if I don't go now, I may never have another opportunity. I don't know what I'll find but I need to try. I feel a desperate ache in my stomach telling me I need to reach out to them. This might be my last time. I can't help how I feel."

She looked at him in anguish. Jacob stared at May-Lynn a long time before he spoke

"I know how you feel, girl. I've been scared to go back home for fear of what I may or may not find. I haven't heard from anyone since we got the news about your husband. After that situation I reached out to some of my kinfolk. They were all doing good at the time, just suffering like we are up here, trying to work and feed themselves. It's just bad all over."

May-Lynn looked at him as he talked. She was begging him with her eyes, asking his permission. Jacob spoke.

"How are you going to get down there do you have a ticket? I can help you with that if you need me too. When do you want to leave?"

May-Lynn excitedly answered.

"I already have my ticket, thank you for wanting to help me. I want to leave next week I already checked the schedule. There's a train leaving Wednesday morning at 10:00 a.m. I should get there late Wednesday night or early Thursday morning."

"What about the children? This is the end of the summer and they'll be going back to school in a few weeks."

"I know that, that's why I want to leave next week. I hope to be back by the first week of school, and I was hoping they could stay with you and Ma Ellen to keep an eye on them. I don't want them staying in the apartment alone."

She looked at Jacob expectantly.

"Of course! They can stay with us. These streets are too rough for a few teenagers to be running around the streets of Chicago. No problem at all."

May-Lynn, stood up and gave Jacob a great big hug.

"I don't know what I would do without you and Ma Ellen. You people have been so good to me. I if I've never said it before, thank you, thank you, thank you, I love you and may God continue to bless you."

Jacob smiled and said.
"Your'e so very welcome, and we love you too."

Ma Ellen stepped out on the porch and called everyone in to eat.

SEVENTEEN

MAY-LYNN SEEKING JOHN DAVID

Olivia was very disturbed about her mother leaving, and the night before while May-Lynn packed her bags, Olivia sat on her mother's bed and looked at her.

"Mama can I come with you? I don't want you leaving us up here, even though we're staying with Jacob and Ma Ellen. I'm really going to miss you."

May-Lynn looked at her daughter and sat down beside her.
"Baby I'm not going to be gone that long. I'll be back before you know it. Where's John Jr?"

"He's in the front looking at magazines. You know he's mad. He said we should go down south together. He doesn't like living here in Chicago. I'm glad we'll be staying with Jacob - he listens to him. He never listens to me."

May-Lynn looked out the window at the sun going down over the buildings.

"Yes! I know John Jr. is have a hard time adjusting to all of this, the way we live, going to school. He's a very angry boy, and I don't know how to help him. I just keep praying for him and all of us that things will be alright."

May-Lynn stood and continued to pack. Olivia looked longingly at her mother hoping she could change her mind about leaving, but she couldn't, this was something May-Lynn had to do.The next morning everyone took the trolley down to the train station to see May-Lynn off. She kissed John and Olivia and boarded the train. May-Lynn took a seat next to the window so she could continue waving to her family. Olivia looked longingly at her mother missing her already, she noticed a man sitting in another seat, sitting not too far from her mother.

He was a Negro, and he was looking at Olivia. He lifted his hand and he waved at her. As she looked closer, he kept appearing and disappearing. He smiled at her and she saw him pronounce her name. O-L-I -V-I-A.   She gasped recognizing her father. She remembered him from her visions and dreams. As the train slowly pulled away from the station John David lifted his hand and blew Olivia a kiss. Then she saw her father get up and sit next to her mother.

The next morning Olivia woke up not remembering what had happened on that day. She looked around in confusion, then she remembered that she and John Jr. were staying with Jacob and Ma Ellen while their mother was gone. A sinking feeling engulfed Olivia, she sat up with a start, her stomach ached as she realized that she may never see her mother again.

May-Lynn traveled through the night. She tried to sleep, but she kept having dreams. Dreams about her childhood, living with her mother and father. She remembered the little house where she grew up. She remembered how her mother would cook dinners for her and her father. Those were happy times. May-Lynn didn't know what would be waiting for her in Mississippi, but she needed to see her parents and she had to see where John David died, so her soul could be at rest.

May-Lynn sat up in her seat. It was pitch dark. Except for the stars and the moon there was no light. The train rumbled down the track at a steady speed, turning the landscape into a blur. May-Lynn looked around her there were not many passengers in this car and the few around her slept. She suddenly realized that she was hungry. She reached into the paper sack Ma Ellen had given her and took out a container of cold chicken and some potato salad. She ate quietly, trying not to disturb anyone around her.

She thought of Olivia and John Jr. and a dark sadness enveloped her. She started questioning the trip. Why was she going back to where everything started? Was she in so much turmoil about John David? No longer hungry she put her food back in the bag. She sat looking out the window. Day light was slowly appearing, where the land and the sky met. The half sun had an orange glow that lit up the sky. May-Lynn continued to stare out the window. She felt her eyes closing and soon she fell into a deep sleep.

May-Lynn slept until she heard the conductor announce:

"Next stop Clarksdale Mississippi, in 30 minutes."

May-Lynn sat up and looked around. It was mid-afternoon, maybe 3 o'clock. She stood and went to the dingy bathroom at the end of the car. While walking down the aisle trying to keep her balance, she noticed a Negro, man sitting by himself close to the end of the car. She glanced over at him because he looked familiar. He didn't look up but continued to stare out the window. The bathroom smelled of urine and humane waste. This was how Negros had to travel these days. They were given the worse cars and the substandard conditions, yet they paid the same price as the white folks. She left the bathroom without using it, hoping she would be able to make it the rest of the trip. While walking back to her seat, she notices that the Negro man had moved his seat now to where he could look at anyone coming down the aisle.

As she passed by, he looked up at her and smiled. She stared at him trying to recall where she knew him from. As she passed him, she heard him call her name.

"May-Lynn!"

She stopped and turn to look at him, but he was gone. May-Lynn rushed back to her seat. She sat down and begin to shake. No matter what she did she couldn't stop her hands from moving. A sudden dread came over her, she should have never left her children in Chicago. Her worst fear is that she would never see them again.

EIGHTEEN

BACK IN MISSISSIPPI

May-Lynn stepped off the train in Clarksdale. The town looked the same. It was 3:30 in the afternoon. The few stores and shops were getting ready to close. People were going home to have supper. She left the Train Depot and walked over to the local drug store. When she opened the door, she saw a negro man sweeping in the back of the store. He didn't look up at her, but he did call her name.

"I've been waiting on you May-Lynn. I'm glad you made it."

He stopped sweeping and looked up and smiled at May-Lynn. She stepped closer to look at this stranger. She didn't recognize him, she'd never seen him before, and she wondered how he knew her name. He finished sweeping, picked up the trash and put the broom away. He walked over to May-Lynn and smiled. He reached for an old tattered coat and hat that was a hook on the door. While putting on his coat, he asked May-Lynn.

"Are you ready to go?"

"Who are you and how do you know me?"

The old gentleman looked at her with compassion in his eyes.

"Young lady this is all a part of your life. And I'm here to help make it happen. The African Gods are looking from above and guiding your road map of life, and they sent me to help."

May-Lynn looked at him in bewilderment.

"What is your name?'

He looked at her in surprise.

"Girl you know me, my name is John."

May-Lynn stared at him in disbelief. She didn't ask any more questions, but quietly followed John out of the door. When they were outside. John quickly turned around and mumbled something.

"Got to lock this door. Master don't like it when I don't lock up. Got to keep my job."

Then he laughed. May-Lynn looked at the street and for the first time noticed a horse and buggy that was not there before. John stood by to help May-Lynn up on the buggy. John handed her the small bag that held her belongings. He then went around and climbed in beside her. He clucked on the reins and the horse slowly started walking down the street. The buggy moved through the town.

May-Lynn saw candles lighting the small windows, where people lived with their families. As they reached to outskirts of town, the roads became very dark. The light of the full moon allowed John to see the road ahead. They passed a few plantations that stood dark and lifeless off from the road. The slave quarters surrounding the plantations appeared to show some life. May-Lynn realized not all former slaves left their homesteads, and many stayed on to work as sharecroppers. That reminded her of John David, and how Mr. Johnson forced them to work without pay. That was the main reason they left Mississippi.

John continued to lead them down the dark road. May-Lynn looked ahead, and she saw on her right, a small cottage, about five feet from the road. There was a light that illuminated around the cottage, and it sat on the patch of land as if it had been placed there by another force. The buggy slowed down as they approached the cottage. John pulled the reigns on the horse and it stopped. John turned and looked silently at May-Lynn, then he nodded toward the house.

"They're in there waiting for you.

Go on in and don't be afraid.

Everything gonna be okay."

May-Lynn looked at John not really believing what he said. She turned to look at the cottage. The light in the window welcomed her to see what was inside. She slowly got down from the buggy. John handed her, her small bag. She started walking toward the small porch and decided to tell John thank you, but when she looked back John, the buggy, and the horse were gone. She looked down the road and didn't see anything. It was as if they never existed. She turned back to the house and saw that the door was open. In the door stood a small woman who called out to her.

"May-Lynn is that you?"

May-Lynn started to run to the voice that was so familiar.

"Yes! mama it's me, it's really me. I've come back to see you."

The little woman ran to the edge of the porch, and when May-Lynn reached the steps her mother reached out her arms to her daughter. May-Lynn stood on the porch and embraced her mother. They both cried and kissed each other.

"Baby let's get into this house before we catch a cold."
May-Lynn laughed.

"Ok! Mama."

Martha led the way into the small cottage. May-Lynn stepped into the door, looking around. She was trying to if the room looked like this when she was little, but she couldn't remember. She looked at her mother who was smiling at her.

"I can't believe you've come back home. Come on baby and tell where you've been and what you been doing. Tell me about my grandchildren, Olivia and John Jr."

May-Lynn looked at her mother in surprise.

"How did you know....."

She trailed off when her mother put up her hand to silence her.

"Now daughter, you know if anything about me, you know that I see what you see. I hear what you hear, and I know what you know. I know when you left, I know that you had to run away in the night. I know that John David didn't go with you, and I know that

John David is dead. And for that I'm so sorry. And now daughter I want to know why did you come back here? Why are you here, there's nothing here for you?"

May-Lynn stared at her mother.

"Mama what are you asking me? I came back to see you and daddy. I left without saying good-bye, and I felt bad for that. So of course, I came to see about y'all."

May-Lynn looked away from her mother, as if she was ashamed. She went to sit down on the old couch which sat in the middle of the living room. Martha came and sat down beside her daughter.

"Daughter I'm glad you came back, but I don't know if it was a good idea. This place holds a lot of bad memories for you. But of course, you know I'm glad to see you."

She reached over and gave May-Lynn a hug. May-Lynn hugged her mother back holding her tight and afraid to let go. After awhile she released her and looked into her eyes.

"Mama! Where is Daddy? Is he in town or visiting somebody?"

Martha turned away from her daughter and stood up. She walked over to the hearth picked up a stick and stirred the burning wood. She didn't look at May-Lynn for a long time. When she turned back May-Lynn could see a yellow glow surrounding her mother's head. Martha spoke with sadness in her voice.

"Baby your daddy died last year during the cold winter."

May-Lynn gasped.

"How come nobody came to get me. Mama if you knew where I was, how come you didn't send for me? I could have come back. Specially to see about my daddy."

Martha looked at her:

"Baby you couldn't do nothing, he caught a bad virus and the doctor gave him a few days to live, then he was gone. Nobody could save him. It was his time."

Martha walked back over to where her daughter sat. She reached out her hand making her stand up.

"Your daddy loved you and you love him. You knew it and he knew it. And that's what count. Now come on in the kitchen and get something to eat. They ain't feeding y'all up in Chicago? Girl you're skin and bones."

In spite of herself May-Lynn laughed at her mother. They went into the small kitchen. Where Martha had cooked greens with salt pork, cornbread, and fried chicken. May-Lynn looked at the meal and asked her mother.

"Were you expecting somebody else? This is a lot of food."

"The person who I was expecting is already here, you dear. I told you I see, hear and know before it happens. I've been waiting for you."

May-Lynn asked no more questions, remembering that she was very hungry. She sat down in the small wooden chair and waited as her mother fixed her plate, heaping with food. Then Martha too sat down at the table, May-Lynn noticed that her mother didn't fix herself a plate.

"Mama aren't you gonna eat?"

"No baby it's just a joy to sit here and watch you. It's so good to have you here. Now tell me more about Olivia and John Jr."

May-Lynn put her fork down missing her children.

"Olivia is wise for her age. I guess you know she has the gift. It came on her the day I found out John David was killed. She's been having visions ever since. I don't worry about, Olivia she's a survivor and she knows what it takes to live in this world."

May-Lynn's face turned dark.

"But mama I'm worried about John Jr. He's a very angry boy. Short tempered. He doesn't like school, and when he does go, he gets into fights with the other boys. Oh, mama he loves money, and every opportunity he tries to get it. He works with Jacob. That's right you don't know Jacob, do you?"

Martha looked at May-Lynn.

"Child! I know about Jacob and Ma Ellen. Those people are you guardian angels. They were sent ahead to Chicago by the Gods to protect you, Olivia, and John Jr."

"So Mama is you saying that everything I've gone through was supposed to happen?"

Martha stood and took May-Lynn's plate to the sink.

"I'm saying that some gifts can be controlled, and some have to be watched very carefully. Olivia have the gift of foresight, but she will not always be able to control the future. John Jr. is an angry boy, and he will stay that way for the rest of his life. Losing his father and the fast life of the city will take over his soul."

Martha turned from the sink, and her eyes clouded over. She looked back at May-Lynn with sadness in her voice.

"You won't be able to save John Jr. No one will. Baby I'm tired, I'm going up to bed. You turn the candle down when you ready to go to sleep. Love you baby girl and thanks for coming to see about your mama."

Martha left the kitchen humming one of her favorite hymns. " *I'm gonna fly away, I'm gonna fly away, to see my lord."*

"Praise God!"

May-Lynn sat down in one of the old kitchen chairs. She thought about everything her mother had told her. She couldn't believe that her daddy was gone. She missed him so much. She laid her head on the metal topped table, welcoming the coolness to her forehead. Too tired to go upstairs May-Lynn drifted off to sleep.

May-Lynn woke the next morning with the sun shining brightly through the small kitchen window. The sun felt good on her face. She stood and walked over to the window, she placed her hands on the pane that was starting turn hot from the sun's rays. She turned and looked around the kitchen. A dirty dish was still on the table she looked at it in surprise remembering that her mother had taken the dishes to the sink last night.

She walked over to the sink and saw no dishes there. May-Lynn started to get a strange feeling about where she was and visiting her mother. May-Lynn left the kitchen to go check on her mother. While passing the living room she saw that all the furniture was covered with white cotton sheets. This is not what she saw last night. She went to the stairs and called out to her mother.

"Mama! Mama! Are you woke?"

May-Lynn went to the first bedroom at the top of the stairs. The door was partially open. May-Lynn pushed the door open to a dark room. She called out.

"Mama! Mama!"

No one answered. She walked into the room to turn on the light by the nightstand. The room luminated with light. May-Lynn looked around. She saw the bed where her parents had slept. It appeared no one had slept there in a long time. It was neatly made, with the quilted bedspread that her mother cherished. All of the other furniture in the room was covered with sheets like downstairs. May-Lynn sat down on the bed wondering where her mother had gone.

She looked at the old fashion clock on the nightstand. The time said 8:00. Where was her mother at this time in the morning? She noticed the little drawer on the nightstand partially open. When she pulled open to look inside, she saw a small red velvet bad and some papers. She pulled the bag out and set it on the bed, she then picked up the papers and started to read. The first one was a funeral announcement about her father. She picked it up and looked at the picture, of her dad. His sat in a chair, with his hands folded. He looked stern and proud. And there appeared to be a twinkle in his eyes. She held the paper to her heart and whispered.

"I'll always love you daddy."

She placed the paper back on the bed and picked up another funeral program. She looked closely at the women in the photo. May-Lynn screamed and the paper fell to the floor. She stared at the photograph, which started to grow in size. She looked into the face of her mother. The funeral program was her mother's. May-Lynn jumped up and ran from the room. She went downstairs and out the front door. She stood in the yard and screamed. What was happening? She saw her mother last night, and now a paper was stating that she had died. May-Lynn fell to the ground and wept. She wasn't sure how long she laid on the ground, but she felt a hand trying to help her stand to her feet. She looked up and saw Negro man with a full beard. She pulled away and started to run but he spoke, and she remembered the voice.

"Ms. May-Lynn! Ms. May-Lynn! Don't be afraid it's me Jonas."

She stopped struggling and stood up. She looked at this man shabbily dressed, in torn and tattered clothes. As she looked closer, she could tell that the beard made him look older than his years. He spoke again.

"Ms. May-Lynn you don't recognize me? It's me Jonas. I worked for your mama and papa many years. Don't you recognize?"

May-Lynn found her voice.

"I remember you. You worked in the fields for my daddy. But what are you doing here I thought you had left a long time ago? Even before I ran off and married John David."

"I did leave and when I saw nothing was out there for me, I came back. Been here ever since."

May-Lynn spoke in a frighten voice.

"I came here last night to visit my mama and daddy. When I got here my mama with her own hands opened the door. I went into the house and we talked, laughed and cried together. I was able to touch her face and smell her scent. She was here I tell you."

Then May-Lynn started crying.

"But I was just upstairs, and I saw a funeral program and on that program was a picture of my mama. That paper showed my mama dead. Now is she dead or alive? Tell me I need to know."

Jonas looked at May-Lynn with sadness in his eyes.

"Yo daddy died last year, November and yo Mama, died on Christmas Day. I don't know who you saw last night, but it couldn't been yo mama."

"But I did see her. She talked to me and she fed me."

May-Lynn said with a smile. She then started walking back to the house. Jonas followed close behind. She ran in the door and looked around. With Jonas coming in behind her she told him.

"When I came in last night the furniture was not covered. Mama and I sat on the couch. We talked about me and John David, and she knew all about my children who are still in Chicago. She was here I know I saw her. I don't know what's happening now I'm so confused."

She then slumped down on the sheet covered couch. Jonas stood by and looked at her, suddenly feeling sorry for Martha's daughter.

"I've been taking care this place since yo mama and daddy died. Yo mama told me I could have this house and all the land. That was her way of thanking me, for staying on and helping them for so many years. Ms. May-Lynn I can tell you one thing."

Jonas sat down on one of the dusty chairs.
"Sometimes yo mama visits me."

May-Lynn looked at him in surprise.
"What do you mean? Visits you?"

He continued.

Sometimes when I'm sleep, I'll wake up and she be standing at the bottom of my bed. Then she'll talk to me. She'll warn me about things happening round here. Like the patrollers coming around. They still treat folks down here like we lower than dogs. There's been a lot of lynchings, down here. White folks mad cause some of us got more than they have. Them crackers a few times have come around trying to take this house and the land. But I sit on the porch with you daddy's gun and tell them I'll blow them
away if they don't go. But they keep trying. Well yo mama came to me a few weeks ago telling me about yo visit. She wanted me to give you a mess..."

Jonas stood up the room became dark, a yellow cloud appeared, covering him from head to toe. When the cloud cleared, May-Lynn saw her mother. May-Lynn stood up and hurried toward her. But Martha held up her hand forcing May-Lynn to stop in her tracks.

"You can't touch me baby, my body is wrapped up in the spirit."
"Mama I touched you last night, I talked to you last night. How did I do that if you're dead?"

May-Lynn's voice became sad, as she realized that her mother was gone, and she would never see her in human form again.

"Baby I had to come see you last night because you needed to know that even though I or your daddy was no longer here, we still loved you."

"I love you too mama, I'm just so sad that I didn't visit you and daddy sooner."

"Baby you couldn't have stopped this. It was going to happen whether you was here or not. Everything happening now was utabiri (PREDESTINATION). Our lives was a pre-written script, wrote a long time ago. And we can't change any of it. Baby I've never tried to tell you what or what not to do, but you being here is not good. I know you wanted to get close to John David, but that's not the best for you or your children. Did John David summons you here?"

May-Lynn turned her head away from her mother. Then she turned and spoke.
"No! He didn't want me to come here. But I knew I had to come. I'm up in Chicago and I can't live without knowing where he died. His grave called me here. I had to see it for myself. The place where he died. I need to go there to get a piece of myself back. So, I can live and take care of my children."

Martha looked at her child, shook her head.

"That swamp has nothing for you. Nothing but death and grief. You need to go back to Chicago and save your children because they need you. John David is back with our Fore Father's in Africa, where he belongs. Go home my daughter."

With those words, Martha the yellow cloud appeared again and May-Lynn's mother was gone. May-Lynn knew that she would never see her again. Jonas was standing in the same spot looking dazed. Then he spoke finishing the word MESSAGE .

"She wanted you to go back home and take care of Olivia and John Jr. She said coming here was a very bad idea."

He stopped talking and looked around the room.

"So, are you gonna do what your mama said?"

May-Lynn looked at Jonas.

"Yes! I'm going back, but can look around this place and take something back, that reminds me of my mama and papa?"

"Sho you can! I ain't touched nothing since she died. I left everything the way she left it."

"Thank you!"

As May-Lynn headed for the steps, she wanted to take the things she'd found in the nightstand. Walking into the bedroom, she located the small leather pouch, and the funeral programs stacked neatly beside the pouch. She sat down, carefully folded the programs and placed them on the side. She then picked up the leather pouch. She untied the leather strap and poured the contents onto the bed. Inside were five items. A smooth transparent yellow stone, a bird's feather, the tooth from a wild animal, a clump of hair, and a broken glass mirror.

May-Lynn picked up the mirror and looked in it. Instead of seeing a reflection of herself she saw the woods. Looking closer, she was able to see beyond the trees. She heard sounds, the wind blowing, birds chirping, and when she placed the glass to her ear, she heard water from a rushing stream. Out the corner of her eye she saw the yellow stone starting to glow. She picked it up and looked closer. She saw a body of water and in the water was the face of John David.

NINETEEN

THE GIFTS ARE REVEALED

May-Lynn sat on the bed shaking, she stood up gathered the items and put them back into the pouch, she then put the pouch in her skirt pocket for safe keeping. She left the bedroom and went downstairs. Jonas was standing at the bottom of the steps looking expectedly at her.

"Was you able to get what you came here for?"

He said quietly. May-Lynn looked at him and answered.

"Yes! I have all I need. I'm going to leave now."

"Do you need a ride back to town."

"No! I'll be alright. Thank you for everything Jonas. You made a promise to my parents, and you've kept this place since they've been gone. And you can have all of this, the land the house, you deserve it. I don't have a need for it. I won't be back."

Jonas looked at May-Lynn.

"Well thank you. And I appreciate it. I've enjoyed taking care of this place. It's like home to me. And without your folks helping me a long time ago. I don't know where I'd be now. I truly loved them. They treated me like a son."

May-Lynn looked at him and walked over to give him a hug. He felt warm as she put her hands around his neck. She then turned and picked up her bag and left her parents house. She walked out of the yard to the gate that led to the road. Before starting down the road she stopped and looked back one last time at the house where she grew up.

She stopped in her tracks and stared at an empty lot. She ran back in the yard. Yellow smoke started to rise from the spot where the house stood. As the smoke rose higher and higher. May-Lynn could see and hear images in the smoke. She heard laughter, crying and the faces of adults and children.   As she continued to watch, the smoke started descending back to the ground, and disappeared. May-Lynn causelessly walked up to a small mound of yellow dirt.

Perched in the middle of the mound sat a Dove. It was purring and looking at her. Its eyes were yellow, and its feathers was a golden bronze. When May-Lynn stepped closer to get a better look the bird sat up, its wings expanded, and it slowly flew into the air. It hovered over her looking down, then it suddenly took off flying above the road. She didn't know what caused her feet to move, but she found herself hurrying to follow the bird. She ran out of the yard and trotted down the road, keeping the bird in her sight. She stumbled over rocks and sticks trying not to fall, but she kept her eyes on the Dove as it soared in the sky under the bright sun.

About a half mile down the road the Dove landed on the branch of a tree, on the side of the road, May-Lynn stopped also. She was tired and she sat down in the to rest. She looked up at the Dove as it sat quietly in the tree. What was she supposed to do now? It quietly sat purring and watching her. She stood up and moved closer to the tree. This tree was bare and showed no signs of life, except for the Dove. She stepped closer and looked intently in the Dove's eyes, and they showed nothing. Then the Dove suddenly turned its head toward the woods. May-Lynn also turned her head to see what she could see, she heard the sound of water, like a rushing river falling over rocks. A narrow path lead into the woods and May-Lynn decided to follow it. After taking a few steps she remembered the Dove and looked back to see if it was still there, but the Dove and the tree was gone.

May-Lynn walk deeper into the woods, following the winding turns of the path. She ventured deeper into the woods, stepping over huge rocks and fallen branches. The woods were eerily quiet, but the sound of the water was getting louder. She soon stepped into a clearing and stood on the bank of a river. She stood and looked across this body of water that appeared to be about a half mile to the other side. She didn't know if she was supposed to cross the river. And if she did how would she get to the other side. May-Lynn stood at the edge of the river not knowing what to do next. She felt a vibration in her skirt, she then remembered the pouch with the items she had taken for her parent's house. She reached in her pocket and took out the pouch. While holding it in her hand, she noticed something was glowing from inside the pouch.

She opened it up and reached inside. She sat down on the riverbank and examined the items from the pouch. She took out the clump of hair, the animal tooth, the glass mirror, the birds feather and the yellow transparent stone. She carefully laid the items on a flat rock that was nearby. She picked up and examined each item. She first picked up the CLUMP OF HAIR, she carefully tried to separate the hairs, as she pulled and pulled all of a sudden, the hair started to dissolve as if it was on fire. May-Lynn watched as it turned to dust. Next she picked up the ANIMAL'S TOOTH, and turned it over and over in her hand, she was now afraid to pick up the other items, for fear of destroying them. Apparently, these items were placed in her care because they have a great meaning in her life.

She looked over at the BIRDS FEATHER, and picked it up, while examining it closer she noticed that the color had changed from white to a golden bronze, the same color as the Dove. She put the feather back on the rock. Then she picked up the Glass Mirror and held it up to her face. The reflection was cloudy but as it started to clear May-Lynn gasped when she saw a small house that looked familiar. It was Jacob's and Ma Ellen's house. When looking closer she could see inside the house. May-Lynn was able to look into the kitchen where she saw her children, Olivia, John Jr., Jacob and Ma Ellen. They were sitting at the kitchen table eating dinner. May-Lynn could see them talking and laughing, but she couldn't hear what they were saying, they appeared to be happy.

May-Lynn was suddenly jealous, angry and sad at the same time. She started to cry she missed her children. Why had she left? Why was she here? What was she trying to prove? She quickly put the mirror down not able to look at the family she'd left in Chicago. These were questions she asked herself, but she had no answers. At that moment she made up in her mind that she was going to get back to her family, she just hoped it was not too late.

May-Lynn continued to sit on the riverbank trying to decide what to do next. If she started walking now, she could possibly get to the train station before dark. May-Lynn stood and looked up at the sky, with the sun directly overhead, it must be about 12:00 noon. May-Lynn picked up the items from the pouch and carefully started placing them back inside. She picked up the **Yellow Stone** last, as she held in her hand, it was warm and glowing. She looked closely as it turned different shades of yellow in her hand. May-Lynn felt a stirring under her feet. The ground was starting to shake and move, the river had turned a golden yellow. The river started stirring and a whirlpool form in the middle, causing the waves to go around and round.

The **Yellow Stone** glowed and grew warmer in her hand. As she looked closer, she could see a reflection of the river's waves twirling round and round. All of a sudden there was the sound of a roar coming from the river. May-Lynn looked where the water continued to swirl. There stood John David, he was standing in the mist of the waves. He was looking at her with a passion in his eyes. May-Lynn forgetting where she was started to run out to meet him. As she approached the water's edge, John David held his hand up motioning for her to stop. May-Lynn paused, still looking at her husband.

"John Oh how I've missed you. I had to come see where you left this earth, me and your children. My life is a mess, I can't eat, sleep or be a mother to your children. I'm tormented every day trying to survive your death. It wasn't supposed to be this way. We as a family was to go to Chicago and start a new life. But now Olivia, John Jr. and me are living in Chicago without you. John David it's not fair."

May-Lynn dropped her head and started to cry. John David looked at his wife the only women he's ever loved. He wished he could reach out and hold her but that was not possible. He spoke.

"May-Lynn my darling! You don't know how much I miss holding you, kissing you and telling you I love you. Not being able to see my babies grow up, not being able to protect them from this mean world. I too torment every day. But I now realize that I had to sacrifice my life in order for you and the children to live. It had to be done, it was not my choice, and for that I'm sorry. If we could turn back time, I don't know if anything would have been different. The African Gods have guided us through this journey, and it's too late to turn back. I hope you'll forget about me and start a new life up north. That was always my plan for you and my children. May-Lynn go back to Chicago and raise my children. Continue to help Olivia with her gifts, love John Jr. and guide him through life."

"John David I can't do this by myself. I need you to help me."

"You'll be just fine. I'll be watching over you the whole time. I must go now, you won't see me anymore, may job is done. Take care May-Lynn, and remember I always loved you."

John David started to disappear in a yellow vapor. The vapor started at his feet and continued until it covered his whole body. He stood tall and strong looking at May-Lynn. He smiled at her as his eyes said goodbye.

"Wait! John David don't leave me yet."

May-Lynn yelled out.

She rushed forward and forgetting the slippery riverbank, she slipped and fell into the water. May-Lynn panic trying to reach for anything to grab onto to pull herself on to the shore. The more she flailed her arms she was slowly being pulled down to the bottom of the river. May-Lynn stopped waving her arms as a sense of calm enveloped her. She slowly opened her eyes to look around her. Fishes in brilliant colors of the rainbow swam by and tickled her face, she smiled. Thin ribbons of seaweed floated around her, softly touching her arms and legs. May-Lynn's mind told her not to be afraid. She continued to float down until she was standing on the bottom of the riverbed. She looked ahead and saw three figures floating toward her.

When they got closer May-Lynn recognized her mother and her father. They were holding out their hands to her beckoning for her to come to them. The third figure was John David. He stood back and looked at her. There was sadness on his face. He shook his head turned and floated away. She knows that he was disappointed in her, he never wanted her to come here and he seemed to be saying that now she could never go back to their children. May-Lynn reached out and started floating toward John David and her parents disappeared. She reached out her hands trying to catch up to John David, but she never reached him.

All of a sudden May-Lynn felt her lungs filling up with water, she was drowning. She looked up and could see the sky, she reached up trying to swim back to the water surface. She knew it was too late, she was going to die. She would never see her family again and even worse she hadn't listened to John David, and she had lost him also. She closed her eyes and accepted her fate.

TWENTY

THAT MORNING

About a three days later, John Jr. woke up after dreaming about his mother. He remembers seeing her standing on a riverbank, looking at someone who was standing already in the water. A man was holding out his hand telling his mother to come. She was hesitant at first but then she stepped out on the water toward the stranger. She had a peaceful look on her face, while the stranger reached out and took her hand. Then they slowly sank into the water.

The dream forced John from his bed seeking Olivia. When he reached her room, he stood in the doorway looking at his sister sleep. He didn't know how he was going to tell Olivia about the dream. What did it mean? Why was he dreaming about his mother?

He went over and shook his sister.

"Olivia! Olivia! Wake up I had a dream about Mama, wake up!"

Olivia shook him off.

"Leave me alone! John Jr. it's too early."

Then she sat straight up in bed realizing that he mentioned their mother.

"John Jr. What did you say about Mama?

She looked at him and saw something in his eyes. Then she said it.

"Mama's not coming back, is she?"

John looked at his sister in disbelief.

"You know don't you?"

Olivia shook her head up and down.

John Jr. spoke his voice rising.

"How did you know? I had the dream. Did you have a dream too? Olivia what's wrong with you? How do you know so many things?"

Olivia got out of the bed and stood in front of her brother. They'd never had this conversation before. Olivia felt until she knew more about her gift, she would keep it a secret, but with John Jr. asking now she felt he had the right to know.

"Yes! I do have the gifts, gifts of sight and some others that have not been revealed to me yet. I have dreams, where I can see and talk to people who are no longer alive. I've talked to Daddy a few times. He comes to warn me about dangers and other things."

John Jr. looked at Olivia with a question in his eyes.

"Do I have any of these gifts?"

"John Jr. I don't know. I was told it's really strong in girls, but weaker in boys. I received my gift from Mama and Daddy's mama. At first, I didn't know that I had anything, but on the day when we heard daddy had been killed. The gift came on to me real strong, I was floating in the air. What makes it so strange is I didn't remember anything after that day. I started getting visions and dreams at night. I bet we dreamed the same dream at the same time. What was in your dream John?"

Olivia sat back down on the bed and told her brother to sit with her. John sat down beside his sister and told her how he saw their mother standing on the bank of a river. She was looking at man who was telling her to come to him, then she started sinking. Olivia shook her head acknowledging that she had, had the same dream.

"John what do you feel about this dream?"

He walked and stood by the window. Suddenly a cold breeze filled the room. Olivia looked at John Jr. as he turned into his father. John David turned to his daughter and spoke.

"Baby girl, your brother is right, yo mama ain't coming back. I tried to get her to come back to you and John Jr., but her force was so strong, she made up her mind to be where I was, I'm so sorry. You know yo mama and I will always be with you and John Jr. We'll never leave you, just look over yo shoulder, we're always near."

As Olivia continued to look at her father, the cold breeze returned, and John Jr. slowly came back. Olivia grabbed her brother and held him close. Crying in his shoulder she was surprised as to how tall her brother had gotten. It was as if he'd grown overnight and was turning into their father.   She held him out arm's length, looking deep into his eyes, noticing that he had been crying also.

"She loved Daddy more."

John Jr. looked over his shoulder, turned and said.

"And she loved you more than me!"

Olivia looked at her brother in disbelief, at that moment she felt disconnected. John Jr. sadly looked at his sister and left the room. Olivia didn't go after him because she was in shock, about what he'd said. Why would John Jr. think that their mother didn't love him, she loved them both equally. Olivia fought back tears while walking out of the room. She needed to talk to Jacob and Ma Ellen.

She looked over at the clock on the nightstand, it was 7:00 a.m. Ma Ellen would be up making breakfast. Olivia went into the kitchen. Ma Ellen was at the table scrambling eggs. When Olivia entered, Ma Ellen stopped what she was doing. She sat down at the table and motioned Olivia to sit down also. She reached out and took Olivia's hands into hers. Then Ma Ellen started praying:

"Dear Lord and God's from Africa the Mother Land:
I give you this daughter today. Her heart is heavy and she needs the strength to carry on now that her mother is back with you.The road ahead will be long and hard but I hope You will guide her and keep her safe. Lord, let her continue to use her gift for good. And block all demon forces that will lead her down the wrong path. This I pray in Jesus' name."

"You know, don't you Ma Ellen?"
Ma Ellen shook her head, *yes.*

"Yes baby. I'm so sorry, but yes, I dreamed it last night. It woke me up out of my sleep. I saw May-Lynn falling into the river where John David died. I saw her face, she looked like she was at peace. It's as if she knew it was her destiny, she didn't fight it."

Olivia looked at Ma Ellen.

"On the day Mama left, I was afraid for her. I had a feeling would never see her again. The day she got on that train I saw my daddy sitting next to her. I knew then there was nothing I could do to stop her from going. When she got on that train, she was saying a final goodbye to John Jr. and me."

Olivia put her head in her arms and started crying. Ma Ellen went over to Olivia, she grabbed her up into her arms and hugged her tight.

"Baby we're gonna get through this. Don't you worry. You and John Jr. got Jacob and me. We gonna take care of you don't you worry."

While holding Olivia Ma Ellen asked.

"Where's John Jr. does he know?'

Through tear-stained eyes Olivia spoke.

"That's what's really strange. John Jr. came to my room before daybreak and he told me what had happened to mama. I don't know how he knew, but he was acting as if some kind of force was talking through him. He stood there and turned into daddy. Then in Daddy's voice he spoke about mama dying. That's never happened before. It's like with mama and daddy gone the gifts they had is now taking over his body. Ma Ellen he's very angry, he said that mama didn't love us enough to come back and then he said she never loved him at all. What would make him think that?"

Ma Ellen looked at Olivia.

"John Jr's problems are just gettin started. I'm afraid for him. Olivia keep him close to your heart and soul, or you're going to lose him. In the meantime, I'm gonna pray for both of you."

Olivia went over and hugged Ma Ellen.

"Thank you so much Ma Ellen, you and Jacob have been so good to John Jr. and me and we really appreciate it. Thank you again."

Olivia left and went back to her bedroom to get dressed. She passed John Jr.'s room, but he wasn't there. It was strange that he had gotten out early. Instead of going to school today Olivia decided that she and John Jr. needed to plan their next move. When Olivia entered her room, she noticed something on her bed. Examining closer she found a leather pouch; that wasn't there before. She picked up the pouch and sat down, it felt heavy. She untied the string and looked inside, not being able to recognize anything inside, she poured the contents onto the bed.

The contents fell on the quilt: *a yellow stone, a clump of hair, an animals tooth, a glass mirror, and a birds feather.* Olivia looked at all the items wondering what they were and where had they came from. She first picked up the *yellow stone.* It was glowing and felt warm in her hand. She turned it over and over trying to decide what to do with it. She then placed it close to her face, focusing one eye to look
closer. She noticed movement in the stone. Placing it closer she was able to make out a moving figure moving in the stone. It was a boy walking down a street. He was in a neighborhood that looked like the houses in Chicago. The boy was hurrying, almost running. He kept looking behind him. Then he took off running, Olivia shook the stone and saw that someone was chasing the boy.

Olivia couldn't believe that she was seeing all of this. She continued to look trying to see who these individuals were. She held the phone out in front of her now she could actually see the people closer. The boy, being chased, continued to run. She looked closer and gasped -the boy was her brother John Jr. and there was a white man who she didn't know chasing him! Olivia dropped the stone and ran out of the room.

TWENTY-ONE

JOHN JR'S STORY

John Jr. never felt close to his family, his mother and sister, or his father who he didn't really know. As soon as he was old enough to understand what was going on around him. He saw differences between him, his sister, his mother and his father. He remember a little about where he was born, running through the fields and playing outside in front of the cabin where they lived. Those were happy times for him full of innocence. Olivia was responsible for him while his parents worked. His mother working in the big house cooking and cleaning, and his father working in the fields.

At night after supper he would sit with Olivia trying to wait for his father to come home, but he always fell asleep. He would stir in the middle of the night hearing his parents talking about things that he didn't understand. One night he woke up thirsty, wanting a drink of water. He noticed that Olivia was not in bed with him. He looked up and saw his parents sitting by the hearth, Olivia was sitting on their father's lap. They saw that John Jr. was awake and motioned for him to come. He ran quickly to his mother and climbed up on her lap. John David spoke.

"Baby like I said before if we stay here, we ain't never gonna be able to leave. Mr. Johnson is gonna make sure we never be able to pay him everything we owe. This here is just like slavery."

May-Lynn looked at her husband and nodded her head.

"Then we gonna have to leave here soon."

John Jr. was not sure what it all meant but he did understand that something exciting was going to happen and it would include his whole family.

Later that week John Jr. remembered his father coming home and taking him and Olivia over to the big house. It was dark, John David took them to the woods where he told them to sit down by an old oak tree. They were told to be quiet and not make a sound. Then he went to the back door of the Big House, where May-Lynn was working. As Olivia held her brother's hand, they saw their father standing outside the house. Next they saw their mother and father running toward them in the woods.

They started walking quickly away from the big house. Following the stars, staying close to the river. They walked and walked. He remembered being tired and crying, his father picking him up in his strong arms and carried him the rest of the way. They stopped to rest all being very tired. John Jr. looked at the fear on his mother's face. She grabbed her children and held them close. All of a sudden, they heard horses coming down the road. Two white men stopped near where they were hiding and looked through the woods May-Lynn gasped and held on to her children cautioning them to be quiet.

John Jr. saw his father step out into the clearing where the men could see him. He was talking to them; the men pointed their guns at John David motioning that he had to go with them. May-Lynn raised her hand to her mouth to keep from crying out. John David quickly looked back where he had left his family, he mouthed go on and walked away with the men. May-Lynn started crying, the children tried to comfort her, but she continued to weep. They stayed in the woods for what seemed a long time. The children started to fall asleep. John Jr. remembered his mother shaking him and Olivia telling them they had to go.

"Aren't we gonna wait for papa?"
Olivia asked her mother.

May-Lynn shook her head.
"No baby we gonna have to leave him for now.
But he's gonna meet us in Chicago real soon."

May-Lynn stood and guided her children out of their hiding place back to the road. When they reached the road, she looked longingly in the direction where John David was taken. She almost started to cry but shook it off leading her children in the opposite direction toward the train station. May-Lynn didn't know if she would ever see John David again, but what was more important, she had to get her children out of Mississippi.

John Jr. remembers waking up in his mother's arms as they rode the train to Chicago. He didn't have a clue about what or where Chicago was, he was glad that he was with his mother and his sister. As the train whizzed by, he saw things he had never seen before. Small towns with houses close together. No horses or fields of cotton or wheat. He was confused and also very excited. Soon the train started to slow down. It pulled into a dark tunnel, John leaned in close to his mother, feeling afraid. Then the train stopped. May-Lynn gathered their few belongings and led the children off the train. They hurried along with people of all colors and sizes. He had never seen so many people at one time. May-Lynn held her children's hands tightly not letting them go, this was new to her also.

They walked through a large room with a very high ceiling. People were rushing about passing each other without acknowledging anyone. John Jr. noticed that he, his mother, and Olivia got caught in the rush hurrying toward the doors that led outside. May-Lynn stopped in her tracks. They all stood on the sidewalk looking in awe at the buildings and people. May-Lynn not knowing which way to go, guided her children down the street. They stopped when they saw a Negro man dancing and singing. That's how they met Jacob, who went out of his way to help his family.

John Jr. became fond of Jacob. Back in those days he followed Jacob everywhere. He reminded John Jr. of the father he'd left in Mississippi. John Jr. remembered the day when they got the news that his father had been killed. That day everything changed. John Jr. didn't understand death, but it must be really bad because his mother went to her bed and didn't come out for weeks. He remembered seeing his sister rise up off the ground and floating in the air. How did she do that?

John Jr. resented when he and Olivia started school. He discovered after a few weeks that he didn't belong there. His sister was able to excel in all of her courses, but he had a hard time concentrating and the materials were confusing. He sulked in class and didn't pay attention to the teachers. When May-Lynn found them an apartment John Jr. became upset. He didn't understand why they needed to move. The apartment was horrible, with a bathroom in the hallway. He hated it
and found excuses to go see Jacob. He would spend nights with Jacob and Ma Ellen leaving his mother and sister at the apartment alone, but he didn't care.

The day May-Lynn decided to go back to Mississippi brought mixed feelings to John Jr. His relationship with his mother was already strained, and her leaving him and Olivia behind in Chicago didn't make things any better. John David was dead, and she hadn't heard from her parents since she had left, so why did she feel the need to go back? John Jr. was very angry and refused to go to the station, but Jacob convinced him to, so he went reluctantly.

At the station May-Lynn reached out to hug her children. She told Olivia how much she loved her and how she was depending on her to take care of her brother. John Jr. stood back waiting for everything to be over. May-Lynn looked at John Jr. and pulled him into her arms. She held him tight, then she stood back, and looking directly in his eyes spoke these words.

"GESEGDE WEES VERSIGTIG DAAR BUITE"
(Translated: Be careful where you go and who you see.)

John Jr. looked at his mother strangely, backing away from her. She boarded the train, took a seat by the window, and continued wave to her family.   As everyone stood waving John Jr. noticed the man sit right across from his mother. As he looked closer, he saw an older version of himself. As John stared, the man looked directly at him and waved. John then knew he was looking in the face of his father.

TWENTY-TWO

JACOB AND MA ELLEN

Olivia continued to mourn the death of her mother while John Jr. walked around brooding and silent. Jacob and Ma Ellen tried their best to comfort her, but nothing worked. Jacob decided to reach out to John David's relatives, especially John David's cousin, Henry Brown. He went by the house, on Talman where they had visited years ago. When he arrived, he saw that the house was boarded up. Seeking questions, he went next door to ask the neighbors about the family. An older woman answered the door, looking at Jacob.

"May I help you?"

"Yes! Ma'am I'm looking for Henry Brown who used to live here."

The old woman looked past him, up and down the street. Then she looked over her shoulder back into her house.

"They don't live here no mo! Left a month ago, in the middle of the night. Didn't say where they was going just left."

She avoided Jacob's eyes as if she was trying to hide something.

So, Jacob questioned deeper.
"Did you know them?"

The lady looked at him in surprise.
"Yes, I knowed them. I knowed them real good. Especially that wife we cut from the same cloth. Know what I mean?"

Jacob shook his head.
"No ma'am I don't know what you mean."

The old lady laughed.
"I mean she and me know things, and we see things. I know they wasn't gonna be in that house long because of John David."

"How do you know about John David?"

"I knew about John David, before John David knew about himself. But that don't matter now he's gone and so is his wife, May-Lynn. Henry had to leave cause his job was done here. He no longer had a purpose."

Jacob asked.

"You mean he dead?"

"No, he ain't dead, he and his wife got another assignment."

The lady turned and was going back into her house.

"Tell that little girl Olivia to watch out for her brother, there's danger over in Lawndale, better be careful."

She smiled at Jacob.

"You have a nice day now, Ya here?"

Jacob continued to stare at the door after it was closed. He couldn't explain what had just happened, and he figured that he would never see Henry Brown again. Jacob headed down the walkway toward home. He concluded that Olivia and John Jr. would have to live with him and Ma Ellen, because they had no one else. When he got home, he went into the kitchen where Ma Ellen was preparing lunch.

"Baby did you find Henry Brown?"

Jacob shook his head.

"No! The neighbor told me they left about a month ago.
Didn't say where they was going."

Ma Ellen said.

"I guess that answered the question I had."

She looked at her husband and he agreed.

Ma Ellen took a seat at the table.

"You know, those babies are orphans.

They got to stay with us. It's the right thing to do."

Jacob went around the table and bent down to kiss his wife.

"That's why I love you so much woman, you got a good heart.

Is Olivia upstairs?"

Ma Ellen shook her head nodding yes.

"I'll go up and tell her the news.

That's one thing that poor girl won't have to worry about."

Ma Ellen spoke.

"Those poor children have been through so

much I feel so sorry for them."

"That's why God placed them in our lives,

for us to help them, and that's what we gonna do."

Jacob went upstairs and found Olivia sitting on the bed staring into space. He came into the room and sat beside her. Olivia looked at Jacob with sadness on her face.

"Hi! Jacob I was thinking, and John Jr. and I will be moving out in a few days. We're going back to the apartment."

Jacob held up his hand.
"Now just wait one-minute little girl. You and John Jr. ain't going nowhere. You gonna stay here with me and Ma Ellen."

Olivia looked at Jacob in surprise.
"Oh no! you don't have to do that. Mama got a little money saved and if I get a part time job along with John Jr., we'll make it."

"It's already been decided. Ma Ellen and I agree we need you young people to stay here with us, so that we can keep an eye on ya!."

He smiled at Olivia.
*"Don't you worry, ya'll will always have
a place to stay here in our home."*

Olivia started crying, and Jacob patted her back. He stood to leave, and Olivia ran over to him and gave him a hug.

"Thank You Jacob. Thank you so much."

Jacob hugged Olivia back.
"Baby girl you, and yo brother just like family.
And we take care of family."

Olivia went to bed that night grateful that she and her brother had a place to stay. That night she dreamed about her mother. She dreamed that she was in her bedroom sitting in her favorite chair. Then Olivia opened her eyes because she really did hear someone calling her. She sat up in bed and saw her mother across the room sitting in a chair.

"Hello! Olivia my darling."
"Mama, Mama, I knew you would come back to see me.
Oh! I miss you so much."

Olivia got out of the bed and started walking toward May-Lynn. But May-Lynn held up her hand.

"Baby don't come closer, I'm only here in spirit, you can't touch me. I came back to speak to you, because I may never have this opportunity again."

Olivia slowly backed away and sat on the bed. May-Lynn smiled at her daughter.

"I'm so sorry I left you and John Jr. it was in my heart to always return, but when I found your father, I knew I was to stay with him."

"Our African ancestors wrote in the history books, a long time ago what would happen during this time. We all have a purpose in this world. It was decided a long time ago what we have to do while living on this earth. And it was also decided when we would die. Your father and I were born to be with each other throughout eternity. And the sad part is we, we can't change it."

"The Gods also expect us to use our gifts, hopefully to save mankind. When we've finished our assignments, we must leave. When we leave it is important that we leave a piece of ourselves to carry on the gift. Olivia you're that piece of me. You and John Jr. Jacob and Ma Ellen is also a piece of my story. It wasn't an accident that we met Jacob; he was placed here as our guardian angel to watch over us. And he's doing that."

Olivia spoke up.

"Jacob and Ma Ellen are gonna allow us to stay with them. Me and John Jr."

"Baby I know. That was always the plan."

May-Lynn's eyes suddenly turned dark. She stared at Olivia like she was invisible.

"Baby did you find something on your bed."

"Mama what do you mean?"
"Did you find a pouch with some very precious things inside?"

"Yes mama I found the pouch. What is it for?"

"Darling those are your tools for life, guard them with your, heart and soul."

"But I don't know what they mean or how to use them."

"In due time those tools will become very useful, as you need them you will learn how to use them. Carry them with you always, and never let them out of your site."

May-Lynn rose from the chair and looked loving at her daughter.

"I love you Olivia, always remember that. Take care of your brother."

May-Lynn lifted her hand and disappeared in a puff of smoke. Olivia called after her.

"But mama, I still have more questions, don't leave me now, I have to ask you................."

But May-Lynn was gone.

TWENTY-THREE

JOHN JR. AND OLIVIA

O livia caught up with her brother the next morning.

"John Jr. we have a place to stay. Jacob and Ma Ellen said we can stay here with them as long as we want, isn't that nice of them?"

John looked at his sister not showing any excitement.
"That'll be good for you, but I'm gonna get a job and find my own place to live."

Olivia looked at her brother in disbelief.
"Boy you sound crazy. How you gonna get a job and go to school too?"

John turned his head toward the door, expecting an argument.
"I'm dropping out of school; I don't need no school to know how to survive in these streets."

Olivia ran over to John Jr. and grabbed his arm and yelled.

"You ain't droppin out of school. Mama wouldn't want that."

John yanked his arm away and turned to face Olivia.

"Well if you look around, you'll see, Mama ain't here no mo."

Olivia backed away looking at her brother. He was different, there was hair on his face, and his eyes shone like yellow fire, and his voice was deeper.

"John Jr. I know you don't like school, but if you come back, I promise I'll help you with your studies. All we have is each other, and Mama would want us to stay together."

John looked at her sorry for his words, but he wasn't going to change his mind.

"Hey! John I was going over to the apartment to get some of our things. I would really appreciate it if you go with me."

"I ain't got time today. But I'll be available tomorrow."

"Well I've got school tomorrow, but I guess we can go in the afternoon."

"That's ok with me. I'm really sorry about the school thing but I don't belong there. I tried it for years, but I just can't get it, the reading and stuff. I feel I'd be better working and making some real money. And of course, I'll share it with you Olivia. It's my responsibility now to take care of you and I will."

John Jr. spoke.
"I'm glad we moving out of that "hell hole" I never liked it. And I thank Jacob and Ma Ellen for letting us stay here but I'll be moving out on my own. Some of my friends and I are gonna get a place to live. I'm a grown man now."

"So, I guess you made up your mind."
Olivia responded half-heartedly.

John looked at Olivia with sadness in his eyes.
"Yes, I have! I gotta go I'll see you this evening."

Then John Jr. hurried out of the house. Olivia sat down in the nearest chair. Very concerned about what her brother had said. Olivia looked up as Jacob came into the room.

"May I come in?"

Olivia shook her head yes.

"What's happening with John Jr.?"

"Jacob, I don't know who that boy was that just left here. It's like some evil spirit has taken over his body. He's planning on dropping out of school and getting a job. Then he said he was gonna move out and live with his friends."

Jacob looked at Olivia and shook his head.

"He's a boy, trying to be a man, and he wants to get his own way. All we can do is pray for him, that the lord keeps him safe."

"I guess your right Jacob, but I sho miss Mama she was the only one that could control John Jr. and now that she's gone, he's surely gonna do what he wants, and I can't stop him. Well I'm not gonna worry about, for now."

"I have to get over to the tenement and get our things. I asked John to help me, but he said he couldn't."
Jacob said.

"Now don't you try to get all of that stuff by yo self. I'll get Luther to help you. He'll drive his truck and we'll make one stop and get everything. Let me go call him now."

Jacob and Luther took Olivia over to the tenement to get her things. She only chose things that were personal and precious to her and John. She selected a few of her mother's dresses and a yellow shawl, that her mother had worn on many cold nights. While waiting for Jacob and Luther to return for another box, she sat down in the old chair by the window and placed her mother's shawl around her shoulders. Wrapping it around her, she started to feel strange. A yellow light filled the room. She felt a warm breeze covering from head to toe, then she fainted. She woke when she felt someone shaking her. She opened her eyes and saw Jacob standing over her.

"Baby girl are you ok?"

Olivia looked around remembering that she was in the small apartment. She stood and looked at Jacob.

"Yes! Jacob I'm ok, I put on mama's shawl and because it smelled like her and felt so good I guess I fell asleep. Are we ready to go?" Jacob said.

"Yes! Got everything packed in the truck.
All you got to do is close up."

Olivia looked around one more time at the place where she lived with her mother. She was glad she was leaving it would have been too painful to stay there.

"Is John Jr. gonna come by and get some of his things?" Jacob asked.

"I don't know Jacob. He really wasn't interested in coming back here. I have the key till the end of the week. I'll ask him, but if he don't want to come back that's ok, I'll leave the key with the landlord. But I'm done with this place, it's too painful to be here."

Olivia picked up the last few things and her mother's shawl. She turned off the only lamp in the room, opened the door and looked back one last time.

"Bye mama!"

When Olivia and Jacob returned Ma Ellen met them at the door. Jacob left the room to call his friend Luther. Olivia went over to the window and looked out as the neighborhood came alive. Children playing, women tending to their gardens and men gathering to talk about the day's events.

Her heart ached knowing that she would never see or touch her mother again. It was going to be tough living without May-Lynn, especially trying to lead John Jr. in the right direction. He was determined not to listen to her and now she felt that he thought that he was too grown to even listen to Jacob. Olivia didn't know what she was going to do concerning her brother.

TWENTY–FOUR

LIFE AFTER MAY-LYNN

I t'd been three years since May-Lynn's death. The year is 1913 Olivia is 17 and John Jr. is 16. Olivia is in her senior year of high school, she's determined to get a diploma, knowing this is what her mother would have wanted. John Jr. had been in and out of school the last year. He finally just dropped out and spent his days hanging with some of his friends in a neighborhood lot.

"Have you seen John Jr. today?"

Ma Ellen answered.
"That boy ain't been around at all. I made some lunch, hoping he would come home to eat but he never showed up. How did it go at the house?"

Olivia looked at Ma Ellen with sadness in her eyes.

"It was hard, but I was able to get some of mama's favorite things. Excuse me I'm going to my room and put these things away."

She left Jacob and Ma Ellen standing their feeling sorry for her. Olivia walked into her room and turned on the light. She took the shawl, folded it and placed it with the pouch in the nightstand. Then she walked over to John Jr. room, opened the door and went inside. She turned on the lamp and looked around. She smiled when she saw that he had made his bed. Mama would be proud. She was about to leave when she saw a piece of paper on the floor.

She picked up and read the contents:

LOOKING FOR STONG ABLE BODIED,

MEN FOR LABOR.

No Experience

Have To, Work Long Hours

SUNDAY thru SATURDAY

$2.00 PER DAY

COME TO

1600 S Albany

Chicago, Illinois

Olivia looked at the paper, she guessed this was what John Jr. wanted to do. She laid the paper on his bed and left the room. John Jr. came in later that night. Jacob was waiting up for him. After coming in the front door, he went to the kitchen to see if Ma Ellen had left something for him to eat. He saw Jacob sitting at the table.

"Hey! John Jr. where you been?"

"Out taking care of some things."

Jacob looked at him trying not to let John see how upset he was. He stood up and went to the icebox, he took out a plate of chicken and placed it on the table. Then he went to the cupboard and took out some bread and placed it on the table. He motioned for John to sit down.

"I guess you hungry, you been out all day, sit down and eat."

John shook his head up and down and sat at the table. Jacob placed the food in front of John Jr. and sat across from him. John was starting to become afraid. Jacob had a look on his face that told John that he was in trouble. Jacob stared into John's eyes.

"EAT!"

John started eating. Jacob stood and walked to exit the kitchen, he turned and looked at John Jr. and spoke.

"Nigga! If you ever come to my house this late again, you find the doe locked. I won't let you disrespect my house do you hear me?"

John looked at Jacob startled. He had never spoke to him that way before. Jacob said it again.

"DID YOU HEAR ME?"

John shook his head up and down scared to death.
"Yes sir!"

"And you clean up the dishes. Ma Ellen likes her kitchen clean."

Then Jacob left the room. John Jr. sat there no longer hungry. He'd never seen Jacob raise his voice or become angry, and he was sorry that he made him that way, after everything they had did for him, his mother, and Olivia. John suddenly felt like crap. He would apologize and asked for forgiveness. He stood up put the food back into the icebox. He carefully washed the dishes and cleaned the table. Then he went upstairs to bed.

The next morning instead of running out of the house to meet his friends. John Jr. went downstairs to have breakfast with Jacob, Ma Ellen and Olivia. Everyone was shocked when came into the kitchen. Ma Ellen went to him and gave him a kiss.

"Boy I ain't seen you in a month of Sunday's, sit down and have some breakfast."

John Jr. took his seat at the table. He looked over at Jacob who was eating quietly.

"Mr. Jacob, I want to apologize for last night. It was wrong of me to come in that late. I'm sorry and it will never happen again."

Jacob looked at John.

"Thank you! Son I hated to be mean to you, but you need to know Chicago is a hard town. And it's especially hard on Negros. You just can't hang out in these streets all times of the night it ain't safe. The devil comes out at night to get little boys like you."

John spoke up.

"I ain't no little boy, I'm a man."

"Well I guess you became a man overnight because a few days ago you were a boy. Son I'm just saying you can get caught up in Chicago's night life and never come out. You got to be careful."

John Jr. just looked at Jacob and thought he don't know what he's talking about. I can take care of myself. Jacob having finished his breakfast got up from the table.

"Well now that you and Olivia are staying here, Ma Ellen and I have to set some rules. You have to respect my house and that means you can't come in after 10:00 p.m. Do you understand?"

John Jr. looked at Jacob.
"Yes! I understand."

"Thank you!" Jacob said.

Jacob and Ma Ellen, left the room. Olivia looked at her brother, disappointed.

"John Jacob and Ma Ellen were nice enough to let us stay here, please don't mess it up. What are you doing all times of the night anyway?"

"Hanging out with my boys. We making plans for our future. We plan to make a lot of money in this city, just you wait and see."

"I saw a flyer up in your room. Are you gonna take that job?"

"I might, but I know about some other jobs too. Working in the stock yards, collecting rags or sweeping up the streets. All of those are good money-making jobs."

"John Jr. you never shouldn't dropped out of school. You ain't gonna get far without an education."

"That school stuff is for you I never belonged there. I couldn't put words together and read like you. It was too hard; I just wasn't getting it. No, I'm better off dropping out."

He looked at his sister, as she looked at him, obviously feeling sorry for him. He was starting to wonder if he was making a mistake. So far, the friends he was counting on to give him a place to stay wasn't coming through. They said he would have to pay something in order to stay with them. He looked around the kitchen. Jacob and Ma Ellen was really good to him and they were not going to charge him and Olivia to stay there. Maybe he needed to rethink some things. He looked back at Olivia as he headed to the door.

"I'm going to check on that job, but I'll be back early. Jacob already told me I can't disrespect his house. So far I don't have a place to stay so I better watch myself."

He went over and gave Olivia a hug. She returned the embrace holding her brother tightly. She let go and looked into his eyes.

"John you be careful out there. Everyone walking down the street ain't your friend. Even though slavery is over, there are still some slave catchers out there hunting for Negros. You be very careful."

John looked at Olivia heeding her warning.

TWENTY-FIVE

THE HOUSE ON 19TH STREET

John took the flyer and headed to the address on Albany Street. His friend who's familiar with Chicago told John to walk down Ogden Ave. toward Douglas Park. It was still morning and a lot of people were still in their houses. He passed the Medill School where Olivia attended, it was still early and students were milling outside waiting for the bell to ring. He crossed over to the other side of the street trying to avoid any of his classmates. However, a boy named Albert saw him and called out.

"Hey! John Jr. wait up."

Albert ran across the street and started talking to John.
"Hey! Man, where you going the school is that way."

"I dropped out!"

"Dropped out! Man, why did you do that?"

John looked embarrassed.

"Because I felt like it. I don't need no school to make money out here. I'm going to see about a job right now. You want to come with me?"

"Hell naw, my old man would kill me. Plus! I want to make something out of my life. It's hard for Negros out here, but it's even harder when you don't get an education. I'm staying in school to make me and my family a better life."
Albert said.

The bell rang, Albert looked at the students getting into line to file into the building.

"Well man, that's me. Good luck to you, I'll see ya around."

Albert ran across the street and hurried in the building. John stood there looking at him. School might be ok for Albert but not for him. He continued down the street, not looking back. When he reached the corner of California and Ogden, he noticed a park that stretched at least three blocks. This must be the Douglas Park his friend had told him about. John was told that a lot of Negros worked in this area during the day. Maids and nannies worked in the big brick Gray Stones, cooking, cleaning and taking care of Children. Men worked outside of the homes, shoveling coal, cutting wood and cleaning up after livestock. These homes were owned by Jews. If you ventured further down on Douglas Blvd. you could see more stately homes, Jewish Synagogues, and schools for Jewish children.

John crossed California and continued to walk down Ogden. He was amazed at how large the park was, he'd never seen anything like it. Trees were planted everywhere with small gardens of flowers, there was even ponds with ducks swimming around. He thought about his mother, she would really like this area, to be able to come to the park, and pick flowers. He became sad knowing that she would never see this.

When he reached Ogden and Sacramento he stopped as an old Model T Ford crossed in front of him. The owner was white, and he wore a strange hat and goggles. John remembered seeing these cars in magazines and he hoped to have one himself one day. After the car rattled down the street giving off a loud explosion, John continued to walk down to Albany Street. When he turned the corner, he saw a huge building that took up most of the block.

He wondered if this was the building where he would see about the job. He crossed the street on the side where the building stood. As he walked along looking in the windows, he saw lots of old people, men, and women. Some were sitting staring out the windows, not smiling or laughing. One old lady with gray hair saw him and waved, he waved back, and she smiled. That lifted his spirits a little knowing he was able to make her smile. He continued down the block until he reached a doorway.

He stopped and looked up, the number on the building read:

JEWISH NURSING HOME

1600 S ALBANY

John went up to the door and opened it. He stepped into a dark entryway with steps leading to another level. He went up the stairs and opened another set of doors. Ahead of him was a small office. John walked inside and was greeted by a young woman sitting behind a desk.

"May I help you?"

"Yes! ma'am I'm, here about the job on this paper."

John took the paper out of his pocket and showed the paper to the young lady. She took the paper and read the information.

"Mr. Johnson put this flyer out he works here. If you have a seat, I'll get him for you."

John took a seat on the hard bench, located in the room. As he sat, he looked around at the many pictures of old Men and women. Some of them were smiling with no teeth in their mouths. But many had a look of sadness and hopelessness. John felt sorry for them, he knew first, hand how it felt to be young, miserable and lonely, but he didn't know how it felt to be old, miserable and lonely. He didn't know any old people, except Jacob and Ma Ellen but they weren't that old. He wondered if he was going to work here, he would soon find out. He continued to sit on the bench and looked up when a tall white man came into the office. John stood up and looked as the man introduced himself.

"Hello! my name is Tom Johnson, what is your name?"

John stood up.
"My name is John Brown."

John noticed the southern accent. Which alarmed him. He knew that after the war a lot of Southerners came from down south to start a new life up north. Unfortunately, some these Southerners still treated Negros like slaves. Expecting them to work for nothing and disrespecting them.

"Ok boy I hear you looking for a job."

"Yes I am."

"Well what can you do?"

"I can do anything. I'm strong and able bodied."

Tom looked at him.

"Where you come from, Boy?"

John wondered why he asked that question?
But he had nothing to hide.

"My folks from Mississippi."

*"Ok! We'll try it out. You work from Sunday to Saturday.
I need you for seven days $1.00 per day."*

John Jr. looked at him.
"The flyer said $2.00 a day."

Tom sneered at John.
*"So, you know how to read, huh, Boy? Ok! $2.00. But I'm gonna
make you earn every penny; do you hear me, Boy?"*

*"Yes! I hear ya! And my name is John. That's what I want to be
called John Jr. I won't answer to the word 'Boy'!'*

Tom stood back like he was going to hit John. And John standing
taller let this man know he wasn't going to be disrespected. Tom turned
around, remembering where he was. He looked at the girl sitting at the
desk who was giving him a disapproving look.

"Ok! John Jr. you're going to be working for me at my home and office. I'll show you where it is. Let's go."

Tom went into a small room and grabbed his coat. When he came back, he informed the clerk that he was going home and would return tomorrow. John followed him out of the building to the street. The day was turning gray with clouds threatening rain. Tom made a right turn and started walking down Albany. As John Jr. followed behind, they passed a school where children were playing in playground equipment. There was big sign on the building that said, Nathaniel Pope Elementary School. Children were playing tag and running around. John didn't see any Negro children among the students, so he came to the conclusion that this was a school for white children only.

Tom Johnson continued down the block till he reached the corner. He then crossed the street and headed toward a group of two-story houses lined up facing the park. Each house was similar in height and style, with stairs leading up to a porch. Tall windows, with dim lights told about the individuals who lived within. Red bricks and tall steeples made the houses belong to each other.

Tom Johnson continued to walk swiftly down the block passing a few of the houses. He then stopped in front of a house located in the middle of the block. He looked back to see if John was coming and then proceeded to walk up the stairs. He went to the front door used a key to open it and walked inside. In the small hallway were two entry doors. He went inside the door on the left and asked John to follow him. John found himself standing in a large sitting room. There was a crystal chandelier hanging from the ceiling. Overstuffed sofas and armchairs. A middle-aged white woman was sitting by the window sewing with a needle and thread. Mr. Johnson went over to her and kissed her cheek.

"How are you doing darling?"

The lady stood up and walk where John stood.
"Is this the boy that's gonna, help out around here?"

"Yes. Gloria, He's the only one who answered the ad."

Gloria looked at John Jr. up and down.
"Where you from, Boy?"

John Jr. looked at the women and answered.
*"My name is John Jr. ma'am, and
my folks and I from Mississippi."*

"John Jr, was your folks slaves?"

John Jr. Looked at the woman in amazement. How dare she ask that question. What difference did it make, and it was none of her business, he looked her square in her eyes and answered.

"I'm not sure about that, but maybe my grandma and grandpa was."

John continued to stare directly at her until she dropped her head and walked away. Mr. Johnson told John Jr. that Gloria was his wife, he also informed him that they had no children. A black maid appeared from the back of the house. John looked at her as she kept her eyes from looking directly at him.

"Ms. Johnson lunch is ready. Where do you want it to be served?"

Gloria looked at the maid and answered.

"Joanna just set it up in the dining room, I'm sure Mr. Johnson is hungry."

Then she dismissed Joanna with a wave. John looked as Joanna went back to the kitchen. Then he turned to Mr. Johnson.

"What will I be doing here?"

Mr. Johnson looked at him and said.

"A little bit of everything. Sweeping up the grounds, I have a few horses out back in the stable, you'll take care of them. Bringing in the coal keep the stoves and fireplace going during the week. You're just an everything BOY, whatever I need you'll do. Come with me."

Mr. Johnson led John out of the room. He stepped across the hall to another door. He opened it and, turned on a gas light. Mr. Johnson proceeded to walk down some stairs. John following him being careful not to fall. When Mr. Johnson reached the bottom step, he reached out and turned on another gas light.

John stepped down into a small lighted area. He was able to see the thick wooden square post that held up the house. The walls were covered in green moss from the dampness outside. The room was cold, the boarded windows allowing cold air to fill the room. The room was filled with old trunks, and boxes. Firewood was stacked over in a corner, with box of coal beside it. Dress mannequins, lamps and mirrors told the tale of another life. John looked at Mr. Johnson.

*"Sir if you don't mind me asking how long,
have you been in Chicago?"*

Mr. Johnson looking at John Jr. spoke.

"Well BOY! I mean John. I came up from Mississippi too, after that Damn war. The war that never shoulda happened. The South was great and mighty. Them Northerns just couldn't leave well enough alone. I lost everything. My daddy had a big house. Took care of you Niggas real good but ya'll wasn't satisfied, made a big fuss. Niggas ruined the South."

John listened to him rant and rave. He stopped talking deciding that he'd said enough.

"Well Mr. Johnson I don't think it would be a good idea for me to work here. First of all, slavery is gone, and I won't work where I'm not respected, and you have a real problem with Negros being free and all. So! I'll just be on my way. Have a good day sir."

John started up the dark stairs. Mr. Johnson looking after him, shouted.

"Wait a minute John, maybe we can work something out. I'm sorry, it's sorta hard for me to realize that those days are no longer. But I also need someone to help me with a business venture, where I gonna make a lot of money. You could be a partner."

John stopped and looked around. He came back down the stairs and stood in front of Mr. Johnson.

"What kind of business?"

"Well we'll talk more about that if you agree to work for me."

John thought about what was being said to him at this time. It wouldn't hurt just to work for Mr. Johnson a little while he could always quit if he didn't like it.

"Ok! I'll give it a try."

He stuck out his hand which Mr. Johnson shook reluctantly.

"When do I start?"

"Tomorrow morning, report here at 8:00 a.m."

John said.

"Ok!"

They walked back upstairs and out on the front porch. Mr. Johnson called out to John.

"Oh! John when you come tomorrow report to the back door. Just use the path on the side of the house."

John looked back at Mr. Johnson, not liking what he heard, but he would question that at another time. He turned and started walking down the street. It took John about thirty minutes to get back to Jacob's house. When he walked in, everyone was in the kitchen. Olivia was doing homework Jacob was reading the paper nd Ma Ellen was making one of her wonderful dinners. They all looked up when he came in.

John sat down in one of the kitchen chairs.

"Well I got a job!"

Everyone looked up. Jacob asked.

"That's good son. What kind of job?"

"I'm working for a Mr. Johnson.
He lives on 19th street over there by Douglas Park."

"That's a ritzy neighborhood, Jewish folks live over there. Got a few of my church ladies who work for some of those folks."
Ma Ellen remarked.

Olivia repeated what Jacob said.

"What will you be doing?"

"A little of everything. Cleaning up the property.
Cutting wood and shoveling coal, you know."

He didn't mention the business deal with Mr. Johnson, that would cause a number of questions he couldn't answer. Olivia looked at him with a question in her eyes.

"Did you say you're working for a Mr. Johnson?"

"Yes!"

"That name sounds so familiar, I'm just trying to remember where I heard it before."

Olivia went back to her homework, looking at her brother with questions in her eyes. Ma Ellen announced that dinner was served, and everybody sat down to eat.Later that night while Olivia was laying in her bed. She was in deep thought about John Jr. She was worried about John Jr. hoping that he was making some good decisions. She still was thinking about who John was working for. The name Johnson sounded so familiar. She kept thinking about her brother as she fell asleep.

Olivia woke up and found herself in a field. It was night-time and the moon was high in the sky. As she looked out, she could see the shadows of houses. Little ones were lined up in a row and in the far distance stood a huge plantation. She started walking in the direction of the small house and as she got closer, she saw that this was the house where she and her family had stayed when she was a little girl.

There was smoke coming out of the chimney and a light in the window. Olivia recognized the old wagon her father used, to pull in fruits and vegetables from the field. Olivia slowly approached the house but paused, when she heard the door open. She immediately recognized her father.

John David stepped out of the cabin and anxiously looked around. Olivia stood back waiting to see what was going to happen next. She heard movement and noticed a white man stumbling down the road headed toward her father. John David saw him also and stood by the door waiting. The man reached John David and spoke to him slurring his words.

"Hey John David, where's your wife. She come back yet?"

John David looked at the man and told him.

"Mr. Johnson, I told you sir. She and the children won't be back till in the morning."

Mr. Johnson looked at John and said,

"You lyin, boy. I know that she and the young'ins are gone. I heard the housemaid talkin' bout it."

Olivia watched as Mr. Johnson came and stood in her father's face. John turned his head as he smelled the liquor on Mr. Johnson's breath. John David backed up trying to decide if he should make a run for it! Mr. Johnson backed John David in the door of the house. He raised his hand and put his finger in his face.

"Listen Nigger! I want your wife back in my house. And I want her there now! You better go get her wherever she is, and bring her back, quick, fast and in a hurry. Or Nigger I'm gonna kill you."

Olivia saw her father grow taller over Mr. Johnson. Then she heard a sound come deep from his throat.

"I told you she be back in the morning. I won't be going there tonight cause it's late!"

Mr. Johnson backed up in shock, suddenly afraid. Then he realized that he was talking to a Nigger, and he wasn't gonna be afraid of no Nigger. He pushed John David and shouted at him.

"Who you yelling at boy? Don't you ever speak to me like that again. You hear me you stupid Nigger."

In slow motion Olivia saw Mr. Johnson reach back and try to punch John David. He missed and fell into him. John David's eyes turned a bright yellow. He pushed Mr. Johnson off of him and screamed. Mr. Johnson fell to the ground. John picked up a branch and started beating Mr. Johnson in the head. Every time he raised the branch he yelled out, growling like an animal.

He soon stopped and looked at what he'd done. Mr. Johnson head was all bashed in. His eyes were bloody and open. John David stood up and looked in the direction where Olivia stood. She doesn't know if he was able to see her and she didn't come out from hiding. John David quickly turned and went back into the cabin. He came out with a small bag and threw it over his shoulder. Then he grabbed Mr. Johnson by his feet and dragged him into the woods. He laid the body near tree and piled branches and leaves all over it until it was completely covered.

Olivia still didn't let John David know that she was there. When he finished, he stood and looked at the spot where Olivia stood. He smiled as if he knew she was there. Then he ran off into the night. Olivia took off after him wanting him to know that she was there, but he was too fast. She kept running through the woods. Trying to jump over a branch Olivia fell to the ground, and bumped her head on a rock, and was knocked unconscious.

Olivia sat up in bed with a start. She groaned in pain feeling her head. As she reached up, she noticed a huge bump growing on her forehead. She slowly got out of bed and went to the bathroom. She turned on the light and looked in the mirror, looking at the bump that was getting bigger by the second. Running cold water in the sink, she soaked one of Ma Ellen's towels and gingerly placed in on her head. She went back to the bedroom and crawled under the covers. She sat in the dark and relived the dream she'd just had. She realized that she'd saw her father murder a man, and that man's name was, MR. JOHNSON.

CHAPTER 26

MR. TOM JOHNSON

Mr. Johnson was his father's name sake; at birth he was christened Tom Johnson. He and his family were born in Mound Bayou, Mississippi, where his grandfather owned slaves. He grew up believing what his father and his grandfather believed, that Negros were inferior to the white man. He believed that they were put on earth to be subservient for the white race. He also believed Negros owed the white race a debt of gratitude for saving them from the God forsaken country of Africa. All that had changed with the Civil War.

After the war Tom's father was able to keep most of the slaves that his grandfather owned allowing them to be sharecroppers. He promised them a place to live and the land that they harvested. But of course, that was a lie. The former slaves were never able to live up to the contracts they'd made with his father. At the end of a year of sharecropping the workers found out that they owed for the place to live, and the land. They were never going to be able to catch up which forced a lot of them to stay on the plantations for years.

Tom remembered his father becoming upset and he would threaten the former slaves, telling them if they didn't pay up, he would have them arrested. Many of the sharecroppers, took their families and left in the middle of the night. They would dodge the Patrollers, take the trains and head North.

Things got worse and Tom's father started drinking. He would start early in the morning and drink during the day. Sometimes he would go out and stand in his empty fields and rant and rave until he fell out. Then Tom and his brothers would go out and carry him back to the house. His parents would stay up arguing, Tom's mother always threatened to take the children and leave. Mr. Johnson would beg her not to, promising that he was going to fix things. But neither of his parents believed it.

Tom remembers one particular night when his father got drunk, he left the house saying that he had to talk to John David. John David was one of a few workers who hadn't left. Tom went to bed glad that his parents wouldn't argue tonight. Tom sat up in his bed feeling that something was wrong. He looked out the window and was able to see that the sun was starting to rise. He crept out of bed and went to his parent's room. He quietly opened the door not wanting to wake them. When he noticed that he was alone, he started to worry. Where was his father?

He went back to his room and put on a robe. He left the house and headed to John David's cabin. When he got there, he found it empty, with no signs of John David or his father. He called out to his father who didn't answer. Then he started walking towards the woods. He came across and area dense with tree branches and leaves. He started walking again when he stumbled over something, he looked down he saw his father lying face down on the ground. Tom fell to his knees hoping that his father had just fallen. When he turned him over, he saw the blood and knew he was dead.

John David had killed Mr. Johnson and had destroyed Tom's family. Soon after a wanderer took the house for back taxes. Not knowing what to do or where to go, Tom his mother and siblings were forced to live in the slave quarters. Tom recalls living in the dirty cabin like the slaves his family had owned. Many nights they would eat food scraps from the big house. On cold nights his family would huddle next to the fireplace to keep warm. Mrs. Johnson became delirious. She would cry and scream and sit in the corner of the cabin, mumbling to herself. Sometimes she would leave the cabin, wandering in the middle of the night. Tom started sleeping in front of the door to protect his mother.

The first winter in the cabin, Tom's mother and his siblings got sick. So sick they had to stay in bed. One morning Tom woke up to his sister shaking him.

"Tom! Tom! Get up I can't wake Mama. Somethings wrong with Mama. I keep shaking her, but she won't get up!"

Tom quickly got up and went to his mother's bed. She was lying on her side and when he turned her over eyes were wide open. She wasn't responsive and he knew she was dead. He woke the other children up and told them about their mother. They cried hard. Tom didn't shed a tear, at least his mother would no longer be sad, she was now at peace.He gathered his family together and buried their mother in the back of the big house in the Family Cemetery. On that day Tom was determined to save the rest of the family. Going back to the cabin he grabbed the few belongings they had and put them in a burlap sack. They put on extra clothes to stay warm, left the cabin and started walking down the road.

Going through some papers that his father had left, he got the name of a cousin that lived in Bay Springs Mississippi. Soon after they started out a wagon pulled beside Tom and his siblings. Tom inquired if he would take them to Bay Springs for a small fee? The stranger said yes. Tom took out his father's watch and gave it to the stranger. When they arrived, the cousin wasn't too happy to see them because of his money problems. But he did allow Toms brothers and sister to stay with him, if they were willing to earn their keep. Tom's plan was to go up North to Chicago. He promised his cousin he would send money back once he found a job.

Tom also hoped to make enough money to buy back his family's house and land. He didn't know how long it would take him, but he was determined not to come back until he reached his goal. His brothers and sister cried at the train station. Tom really didn't know if he would ever see them again, but to him that was not important. He left Mississippi not looking back. Tom arrived in Chicago the next day. He left Union Station and stood in awe looking at all the people and the tall buildings. He didn't know anybody in this city. But he would walk around until he found someone who would help him.

It didn't take a long time for Tom to establish himself in the city. He applied for a job working for the city and got it. He also started socializing with a group of white southern men who had also ventured up North to find a new life. While attending a group meeting, he was introduced to a southern belle, her name was Sarah Mitchell. They started dating and soon got married. Tom quickly forgot the siblings he'd left in Mississippi. He broke his promise and never sent any money to his cousin. He quickly got caught up with the city life. Going to restaurants and shows on the weekends. He also tried to lose his southern accent especially when talking to people who were born in the North. He avoided political conversations, talking about the war and slavery. It's appalled Tom when he saw Negros walking around freely, with good jobs. They were living well up North, and this made him angry.

Tom continued for weeks and months to live in Chicago. He bought a house for him and his wife in North Lawndale. They never had children, but they did lead a pretty decent life even during the depression. After settling in the city, Tom started to revisit the reason why he came to Chicago. Up until now he was able to keep in contact with the man who had bought the family house and farm. He didn't know if he would ever go back there to live, but it wouldn't hurt to use the land to make money. His plan was to recruit workers, especially Negros, to work the land in

Mississippi. In spite of being ignorant they were hard workers.

He would hire one Negro to be the foreman. Then the foreman would recruit other strong men to work for him. He knew during this Depression it was hard to find jobs in Chicago. And saw poor people which included whites and blacks suffering daily to keep food in their family's mouths. He would offer these young boys, money, food and a place to sleep, then he would encourage them go to Mississippi to work and own land, promises that would never be fulfilled.

Tom had tried this scheme when he first came to Chicago, but he soon found out that the Niggers up here were a lot smarter than the ones who worked for his father. They had the nerve to have some education. Shucks! They read. And they had nerve to question him. So many had walked away. Except for one. A boy named Paul Jackson. About two years ago a young Negro named Paul Jackson came to work for him. He was a good worker. He'd come to Chicago, like so many
other Negros hoping for a better life. The good thing was that Paul didn't have any people in Chicago. So, he was going from flop house to flop house. And sometimes he'd sleep on the streets. Tom offered Paul a place to stay, which Paul readily accepted.

Paul worked steadily for Mr. Johnson for six months. They had developed a good relationship. Tom even gave Paul some added duties of making bank deposits and having a key to his house. One day Mr. Johnson had a conversation with Paul, he told him that he wanted to make his Assistant. Paul inquired as to what that meant. Mr. Johnson told Paul how he wanted to start a business that would allow a lot of boys in the city to have jobs. Paul anxiously became interested. He had a lot of friends who needed jobs and if he could help, he would.

It started out with Tom putting Paul in charge of recruiting young men ages 15 to 25. But the most important thing is they had to be poor, homeless and no family. Paul wondered about those qualifications and brought it up to Tom.

"I want to help those that needed it the most. I feel sorry for those young men who have nothing and no one. I want to help them first and then I'll reach out and help others."

Paul looked at Mr. Johnson mulling over what he had said. He still had concerns, but he would play the *"wait and see game"* because he really wanted to help his friends. Paul immediately started recruiting boys for Mr. Johnson. Mr. Johnson knowing that these boys would be working on a farm, turned his backyard into a small garden. He purchased tools of all kind and started training the boys Paul had recruited. He soon found out that some of these boys had never worked in a garden before. So, he had to show them how to prepare the soil, dig rows, and plant different kinds of seeds. They worked hard during the Spring and Summer, and they were rewarded for their efforts in the Fall by having great meals of what they had grown. During the cold months, some of the boys stayed in Mr. Johnson's basement because they had no homes or family. They were happy because they wouldn't have to spend another cold winter outdoors.

Paul was also happy. From what he could see Mr. Johnson was good and kind to his employees. He took care of them during the holidays. By serving big dinners for Thanksgiving and giving bonuses at Christmas. Paul enjoyed being in charge and thankful he could help his friends. All went well the first year. Then Paul noticed Mr. Johnson start to change. He was becoming more demanding. Instead of working a few hours a day he forced the boys to work longer hours, some days they worked from morning till night, stopping for only one meal. After this had gone on for two weeks Paul approached Mr. Johnson and asked what was going on. Mr. Johnson said.

"Paul, I got a cousin in Mississippi and he need some good workers. I'm pushing the boys because this could be a great, opportunity for them to make some good money. My cousin Roy want me to send down my workers down in the next two weeks to help him with his crop. For every acre they help him plant, he's gonna give them a place to live, a living wage, and a half an acre of land. And get this Paul - the more land they help plant, the more land he'll give them to work for themselves. You see, he's ready to give it all up. The war has made him tired and he's just ready to retire and sit back. But he wants to give this land to someone who will take good care of it."

Paul quietly listened to Mr. Johnson trying to understand what he was saying.

"So you telling me that we gonna send all these boys to Mississippi to work on another man's farm?"

"Yes, that's right but they gonna make good money, land, and a place to live. That's a real good deal, don't you think?"

Paul looked a Mr. Johnson in disbelief.
"Mr. Johnson that's sounds like what we Negros just left. Isn't that just sharecropping?"

Mr. Johnson looked at Paul in surprise.
"Of course not, and how do you know about sharecropping? You ain't never been to Mississippi."

Paul noticed that he had hit a nerve.

"Mr. Johnson, I may have never been a sharecropper, but I have relatives who have, and it never turned out good for Negros. Ain't there another way these boys can keep working without going back to Mississippi?"

Mr. Johnson looked at Paul suddenly angry with him. How dare he question him. He would never get away with that if he was in the South.

"Well Paul it's really not up to you to decide. It's up to the men. If they want to do this, I'll send them down there, pay for their tickets and everything, even give them a lunch."

Mr. Johnson walked away. Paul just looked at him as he left the basement of the house and went upstairs. Paul was not trusting this information and the best he could do was warn the workers.

The next couple of days, while working in the garden. Paul idled up to each worker.

"Hey, did Mr. Johnson ask you about going down south to work?"

Most of them said no. Making Paul think that maybe Mr. Johnson had changed his mine. Because he was against it. So, Paul let it go. But one day one of the workers named Simon came to Paul. Simon was a hard worker. When Paul found him, he had been living on the street. Paul offered him a job and he's been dedicated to working hard and making Paul proud of him.

"Mr. Paul are you going with us?"

Paul looked strangely at Simon.

"What are you talking about Boy, go where?"

"We taking a trip down to Mississippi with Mr. Johnson. He told us about working on his cousin's land. Said we can make a lot of money. Said he gonna give us a place to live and some land too. That's why some of us is goin. Some of us never been down to there before. We won't to see what it's like."

Paul looked at Simon, Mr. Johnson did talk to them, he'd even convinced them to go with him to visit. This was not good. These men didn't know what was waiting for them. And he'd heard that the South was worse than before. A group called the KKK was lynching Negros for walking on the wrong side of the street. And Jim Crow was alive and well. White's Only signs were all over the place.

"Simon how many of you goin?"

"Oh just, Willie, Albert, Joe, Allen, Robert and Me."

Paul knew this group they were hungry for money at any cost. But he had to convince them not to go. They would all go down there and never make it back. He would talk to them tonight.

"When ya'll leaving?"

"Leaving at the end of the week. That's why I was going ask you to let me borrow a suitcase to put my clothes in. Got one?"

"Yeah! Man, I got one I'll give it to you."

Paul waited till everyone had settled down for the night. After dinner the workers usually sat around just to "shoot the breeze" they talked about their futures, families and life. Paul cautiously brought the subject of going to Mississippi.

"Simon told me some of you guys are going to Mississippi with Mr. Johnson to look into some work, is that true?"

Most of the workers shook their heads yes. Paul looked around to see their expressions.

"How many of you have been to Mississippi before.?"

Only two raised their hands. And they were not among the ones who were going.

"Ok for those of you who have decided to go. Let me tell you this, when the war ended and slaves was set free, not too many people was happy about that. A lot of them southern crackers lost a lot of money. They lost houses, land and worst of all their slaves. Some of those men ain't got over that yet. I heard a lot of killing is goin on down south. They lynching Negros for anything and everything. Then they have Jim Crow and the KKK."

Simon spoke up.

"*Mr. Paul who is Jim Crow and the KKK?*"

Paul looked at Simon suddenly realizing how naive he was.

"*Son! Jim Crow is a set of laws to keep Negros in their place. And the KKK is a white group of men who hide under sheets. They go out at night and terrorize Negros. They burn crosses and lynch any Negros that they feel have broken the law. They've appointed themselves Judge and Jury.*"

The men looked at Paul, taking in all that he was saying.

"*I can't stop any of you from going. But I warn you to be careful. And at this time, I would warn you to be careful of Mr. Johnson too.*"

And with that said Paul got up, left the men sitting there and went to bed. The men followed and also retired for the night.

In the meantime, Mr. Johnson had been hiding on the steps and had heard everything. He was very angry at Paul. He continued to hide until it was silent. Then he went to Paul's room. He knocked on the door and Paul answered.

"Who's there?"

"It's me Paul. Just want to ask you about some supplies, we'll need tomorrow."

Paul got up and opened the door. He saw Mr. Johnson standing with this strange look on his face.

"Yes Paul! Can you come with me to the back? I need to check on something before sunrise. I want to make sure the men have what they need to do the work tomorrow."

Paul looked at Mr. Johnson with a question on his face.

"Mr. Johnson, we got everything we need for work tomorrow. I already checked it before dinner this evening."

"Well show me so I can take inventory. Just in case we need some more. Come on this won't take long."

Paul still hesitating to put on his pants and shirt and followed Mr. Johnson out of the house. Once they got to the backyard. Mr. Johnson went to the shed and opened the door. e stepped in and waited for Paul. Paul went inside adjusting his eyes to the light. Mr. Johnson closed the door and confronted Paul.

"Now boy why do you want to mess up what I got goin on?"

Paul looked at him suddenly afraid.

"I don't know what you mean Mr. Johnson."

"Boy you know what I mean. You told those boys not to go to Mississippi. I heard you. Now you are playing with my money and that ain't good."

"Mr. Johnson now you know that things ain't good in Mississippi, and those boys would be in a lot of danger. And I just wanted them to know. Now if they decide to still go with you, they can't say that I didn't warn them."

"Well Paul, I don't see it that way. What you gonna do now is go back to those men and tell them that you were wrong. And it would be a good thing for them to go to Mississippi with me. And to make it better you gonna go with me too."

Paul stepped back. He wasn't scared of Mr. Johnson and if he had to defend himself, he would.

"Mr. Johnson this is not the South. And you can no longer treat Negros like slaves. And you sir can't make me do anything."

Paul stepped past Mr. Johnson and was headed back to the house. He knew he could no longer work here so he planned to pack his belongings and leave tonight. Mr. Johnson very upset, picked up a shovel and ran behind Paul.

"Why! You uppity Nigger, how dare you talk to me like that."

Then he hit Paul in the head. Paul fell to the ground and look up at Mr. Johnson in shock. He tried to get up, but Tom Johnson hit him again. This time Paul couldn't get up he laid there unconscious. Tom Johnson lifted that shovel and hit Paul over and over and over. Paul laid there dead. Mr. Johnson shaking dropped the shovel which was covered in blood.

Tom starting to think about what he'd done, he panicked. He remembered this wasn't the south and he could get in trouble for killing a Negro. He had to bury the body. He went to the very back of his house behind the shed. There was a long patch of earth that was not a part of the garden. Tom started digging. The dirt was soft and in no time, he was able to dig a shallow grave. He dropped the shovel and went back to get Paul's body. He stopped! He remembered the body turned on its side, now Paul of on his back and his eyes were wide open. Tom gasped. But he still looked dead. He kneeled down close to his face to see if there was any movement. Satisfied he stood up and grabbed Paul by his feet and dragged him to the hole. He dumped him in and started covering him with dirt. When he finished to make it more secure, he covered the area with heavy stones.

The sun was coming up now. Tom Johnson went back into his house. He was shaking. He went into the bathroom to wash up and clean all the guilty dirt from his body. He was trying to think of a good story to tell the men why Paul was no longer around. They would have questions. He decided to tell them that Paul had found a better job and he wanted them to continue to work for Tom because he was a good man. Satisfied with this explanation he changed his clothes and went to meet the men in the back. When he arrived at the back of the house. He saw that the men had started doing the work for that day. They all looked up when they saw him. Simon was the first to speak.

"Good morning Mr. Johnson."

"Good morning, Simon, Good morning men. How's everybody?" Tom responded, with a smile.

The men responded back and said Morning. Then they all went back to work. Simon walked over to where Tom stood.

"Mr. Johnson, I haven't seen Paul this morning,
have you seen him?"

Tom looked away from Simon trying not to reveal being nervous.

"Why yes, I wanted to talk to you about Paul, because I noticed that you two have become very close. Paul stopped by to talk to me last night. Long after you men were asleep. He wanted to tell me that he was offered another job, and that he would be leaving."

Tom Johnson stopped there to see what kind of response he would get from Simon. Simon looked at him with questions in his eyes.

"Paul told you that he had got another job,
and that he was leaving?"

Simon repeated what Tom had said really not believing his ears. Then he looked away sad and rejected. Then he said in a small voice.

"Wonder why he didn't tell me about this. I thought we was close?"

"Well he told me, and I guess he didn't want to upset you boys, so he wanted me to make the announcement."

Tom cleared his throat.

"Ahem! Men may I have your attention?"

Everyone stopped working and looked up.

"I have an announcement. Unfortunately, Paul is no longer with us. He left early this morning. He has a new job."

They looked around at each other.

"He wanted me to tell you good -bye and to wish you all well. He also said that it would be okay if some of you went down to Mississippi. He believed that you would be safe, and no harm would come to you. And best of all you make a lot of money."

Tom said this last piece with enthusiasm.

"So, get back to work, and I'll call you in for lunch."

The men went back to work. But many looked confused and sad about the news they'd just heard. They all liked Paul, he was like a savior and now he was gone, he had just disappeared without saying good-bye.

Tom called Simon.

"Simon! Before Paul left, he asked me to let you be the foreman. He said that you had the skill and you were a hard worker. So as of today, you're taking Paul's job. And of course, that's more money for you."

"Why thank you sir. I really appreciate it. Thank you! Thank you!" *Simon grinned.*

Then Simon turned and went back to work. He was still grinning until he was no longer facing Mr. Johnson. Simon's mouth turned into a grim line. Mr. Johnson was lying. Something had happened to Paul, something bad and he was going to find out.

TWENTY–SEVEN

JOHN JR'S JOB

The next day John Jr. went to work for Tom Johnson. He went back to the house on 19th street and waited for him on the porch. Mr. Johnson came from in back of the house and saw John Jr.

"So, you're here, and you're early, I like that. Come with me in the back, and I'll show you some of the chores I expect you to do."

John stepped off the porch and followed Tom down the side of the house. He opened a big gate, that led to the backyard. There was junk lying all around the yard. Old wheels, buggies, tree stumps, chopped up wood and broken furniture.

"During the cold months I want wood cut for the fireplace and the stove. That wood over there will last a few weeks then you have to get more firewood from the peddler who comes by once a week. The Coal Man comes every Monday and drops off coal. The men

The men will take it off the wagon and put it in the coal bin. You got to put it in the furnace every morning."

John looked where Mr. Johnson was pointing and noticed a small black door near the basement door.

John nodded as he spoke. Mr. Johnson walked over to a stable. And opened the door. John followed, stood at the door and looked in.

"I used to have a set of horses, but one died, so now I just got Smoky, she's old. But I keep her around because she reminds me of the good old days."

John faced Mr. Johnson and asked.
"Sir what were the good old days?'

Mr. Johnson looked at John Jr. carefully before speaking, then he smiled.

"Boy! The days before the war. I used to live in Mississippi with my daddy. Fore I came up to Chicago. My daddy had a big plantation. He harvested cotton. Had workers who was loyal to him. They loved my, daddy because he took good care of them.
Then after the war everything changed. That damn war messed up everything. Nothing was ever the same."

He looked at John Jr. who was staring back at him. Mr. Johnson stopped talking and led John down the backstairs to the basement door. He took a key out of his pocket and opened the door. They stepped inside and Mr. Johnson turned on a light. They ventured into the basement. John remembered coming down to the basement, the first time he met Mr. Johnson, now he had a better look of what was in this space. It was dark with shadows on the walls. Household items were stored along the walls. John noticed a few locked doors, on one wall. Mr. Johnson went to one door and turned the knob. He stepped in and turned on a bulb in the ceiling. John stood at the door and looked inside. There he saw a small cot with a dirty blanket and pillow. Mr. Johnson turned to John Jr.

"This is where you'll sleep."
John turned to Mr. Johnson.

"Excuse me sir?"
Mr. Johnson repeated what he said.

"I said this is where you'll sleep."

"Sir, I'm not going to sleep here. I have a house on the other side of town. I have a place to stay."
John Jr. said.

Mr. Johnson responded, flustered.

"I thought you understood that I needed live in help?"

"No sir I didn't understand that. I have family that I take care of and I need to be home every night. Now if that's not good enough I can't take the job."

John turned to walk out of the basement. Mr. Johnson called him back.

"Wait a minute. Ok if you can't stay the night then you come to work every day. But the first time you late you're out of here, understand?"

"I understand."

"Ok! I expect you here tomorrow at 7:00 a.m."

John looked at Mr. Johnson.

"No problem! See you in the morning."

John turned and left the basement. He walked out in the cool air feeling conflicted. He doesn't know how he felt about Mr. Johnson. There was something very strange and familiar about this man, but he didn't know what it was. He put it out of his mind and headed toward Jacob and Ma Ellen's house.

When he reached the house, everyone had just finished eating. Ma Ellen welcomed him, and told him she had saved him a plate, that was in the oven. John Jr. didn't see Olivia and figured she was upstairs doing homework. John sat down at the table to eat and Jacob joined him.

"Well how'd the job go?"

John looked at Jacob after taking a bite of Ma Ellen's delicious fried chicken.

"I'll guess it'll be ok. He is strange. I feel something strange inside every time I'm near him. It's like I've met him before in another life. I'm not scared of him, but I'm going to be watching my back, while working for him. He told me his daddy had a big plantation back in Mississippi, and that the war messed everything up for people in the South."

Jacob looked at John and nodded.

"Son some people never expected slavery to end. There were some very angry Plantation owners when the North won the war. It was about economics, power, and money. Without slaves, those white folks lost everything. And the worst thing is they found themselves

on the same level as their slaves. The slaves didn't have nothin and now they didn't have nothin. But worse of all some of those slave owners decided to come up north. They're blending in, but we know different. They brought a lot of their ways up here also. Call you BOY! In a minute. So, you need to be careful around Mr. Johnson, because he ain't what he appears to be."

John stood and took his plate to the sink. He stood there washing his dish and placed in the rack. Then he turned to Jacob.

"He's already called me BOY a few times. I just let it go. But I told him I won't be disrespected. He heard me and still wants me to work for him so I will. One thing though. He wanted me to live there. Showed me some dirty little room to sleep in. I told him I wouldn't be no live-in help. So, with that said I got to be there 7:00 a.m. so I'm goin to bed. Goodnight Jacob."

John turned to leave the room. He hesitated and came back. He looked at Jacob sincerely.

"Jacob I just want to tell you personally that I thank you for letting me and Olivia stay here. You and Ma Ellen helped us the first time you saw us, and I thank you."

John Jr. looked down embarrassed and left the room. When he got upstairs, he noticed a light in Olivia's room. That meant that she was still up. He approached her door and knocked. She answered.

"Come in."

John entered Olivia's room. He saw her concentrating on a page in one of her books. She looked up.

"Hi John. I miss seeing you at school. Are you sure you made the right decision to drop out?"

"I don't know anymore, but I got to try this job thing to make some money. I might go back to school, but not now."

"OK! I won't pressure you anymore about school, that has to be your decision. But I do have to tell you about a dream I had, and it's about the man you're working for. Come sit down. You're working for a Mr. Johnson right."

John sat down and looked at his sister, now very interested in what his sister had to say.

"Yes! his name is Mr. Johnson. How did you know that?"
"And did he come from Mississippi?"

John answered yes.

Olivia sat down on the bed across from John. She started telling him about the dream she'd had about their father. When she finished John stood up and looked at her.

"You think this is the same Mr. Johnson that daddy killed?"

"No, but I think he is related to the same Mr. Johnson that daddy killed."

"So, if he is, what does that have to do with me?"

"I'm just saying I would be careful around him. The spirits tell me he's trouble."

John looked at his sister, appreciating how much he loved her. He went over to Olivia and gave her a big hug.

"I don't say it often, but Olivia I really do love you, and thank you for being a great sister."

Olivia looked at John in surprise, with tears in her eyes she hugged her brother back.

"*John Jr. Brown, I love you too. We only have each other and you can believe I will always be there for you.*"

John said, "*I know,*" and left the room.

TWENTY-EIGHT

TOM JOHNSON AND JOHN JR

I t'd been three months working for Mr. Johnson. John Jr. had tolerated a lot. Tom slipped up and called him boy. He would also yell at John at times for no reason. Fortunately, it didn't happen often, and he would remember to apologize. John was really trying to hold on because he really needed the money. He looked forward to finding a better job.

John Jr. continued to live with Jacob, Ma Ellen and Olivia. He paid weekly into the household expenses. He was forever grateful to Jacob and Ma Ellen, for letting him stay at their house. He recalled bragging about getting his own place. But with the little money he was making that was impossible. Tom had enjoyed having John work for him. The boy was smart, and he worked hard. Sometimes during lunch Tom would go in the basement and eat with John Jr. He'd ask him about his family and where he lived. John told Tom about living with, Jacob and Ma Ellen, and his sister Olivia. But he was very secretive about his father John David and May-Lynn. Something in his spirit to him to keep this story to himself.

One day Tom approached John and asked him if he had any friends that needed a job. John spoke up immediately because he had at least three friends that were looking for job.

"I have a few buddies who would need jobs."

Tom asked who they were and when could he see them. John getting excited said he could round them up in the next few days and bring them to the house. Tom said fine. And went back into the house. John loved the idea that he could help his friends get a job. Seeing his friends daily would be cool. He left after working that day and went looking for his friends. He found them on Roosevelt Road hanging out in the neighborhood lot. It was dark when he got there, somebody had started a fire in the garbage can for warmth. John approached his three friends. And said hello to: Max, Robert and Franklin.

"Hey fellas! How's it going?"

The boys turned to John Jr. and greeted him.
"Hey man! What's happen?"

"You got it dude."

"Hey fellas any of you found jobs yet?"

John Jr. said.

The three shook their heads no.

"Well Tom Johnson who I work for is looking for some
more workers and I told him I'd bring you guys by.
Are you interested?"

Max and Robert said.

"Hell! yeah we interested."

"What about you Franklin?"

"I don't think so. My Pop's cousin is gonna hook me up. I wanna
wait to see how that works out."

"Suits me!" John said.

The group continued to hang out. Smoking, and talking. At ten O'clock. John headed home. He told his friends he would meet them the next morning at 7:30 a.m. He told them to be on time so he wouldn't be late for work.

The next morning John met Max and Robert at the lot. They started walking toward the Mr. Johnson's house in Lawndale. They talked as they walked. John feeling in charge showed his friends the different sights along the way. He was very excited to show them Douglas Park, where the boys stopped and stared in awe. They'd never seen a park this size before. When the reached the house on 19th street, they stared again. They came from meager dwellings. Sharing two to three room apartments with five to six family members.

They walked up on the porch and rang the doorbell. The Negro maid answered the door and stared at the group on the porch. Then she recognized John and said.

"Oh! John it's you. And who's these boys with you?"

"These are my boys. They came to see about a job with Mr. Johnson."

The maid continued to look at them with a
look of disgust on her face.

"Well they ain't gonna walk through this house. So, you got to take them around back."

Then she slammed the door. The group exited the porch and John led them around the back. Mr. Johnson was standing there waiting for them. He introduced himself and shook their hands.

"So, you're friends of John Jr. it's good to meet you.
Did he tell you about the job?"

Robert spoke up:
"Yes! he told us we'd be doing the same thing he does, everyday right?"

Tom looked at Robert and said.

"Yes! Something like that. But I had some other jobs that I thought you boys would be interested in. I got a friend who lives out of town he's looking for some strong young men to help him with his land."

John Jr. spoke up:
"What kind of help?"

Tom looked at him and lifted his eyes in question.
"Well what difference does it make it's a job,
and boys you need jobs right?"

The guys looked at Mr. Johnson and then they looked at John Jr.

John Jr. shook head.

"It's up to you guys, but I know I'm not going out of town to work on anybody's farm."

Then he, went to get his tools to start his job.

Then he turned to Mr. Johnson.

"Do you need my guys? Are you going to hire them?"

Tom looked at John Jr. not liking him much. He felt that he still had time to convince these guys to go to Mississippi.

"Oh! yes I'll hire you guys. In fact, you guys can start today I'll pay you for an eight-hour day. So, get to work." He smiled.

The boys followed John Jr. to the shed and got some tools. He instructed them on what to do. And while they started working, John looked at Mr. Johnson as he went into the house. Something was not right. Why was Mr. Johnson so anxious to send his friends out of Chicago to work? He didn't have the answer, but he intended to investigate to find out.

The group continued to work throughout the day. Tom intending to impress John's friends gave them extra pay. He even invited them to have dinner with him, which surprised John. When Max and Robert agreed to stay to have dinner with Mr. Johnson, John wondered if he should stay also but he decided not to.

His guys were old enough to take care of themselves. So, he left the group and went home. When he arrived at the house, Olivia was sitting at the table eating dinner. Ma Ellen went to hug John Jr. and gave him a big hug. He hugged her back then he asked.

"Hi! Ma Ellen what was that for?"

"Oh! baby I just worry about you so much. Working in that white neighborhood. You just remember to be careful you hear me?"

John smiled at her.
"Yes ma'am. I'll be careful."

Ma Ellen smiled at him and fixed John a plate. He said, *"thank you"* and took his plate and sat next to Olivia. Olivia looked up at her brother and asked.

"How did your day go?"

"Ok! But a little strange."

"What do you mean, strange?"

"Well Mr. Johnson asked me the other day if I had some friends who were looking for work? And of course, I said yes. So, I went by the lot and got Max and Robert to go with me this morning. When we got to Mr. Johnson's house, instead of him asking them to work for him, he wanted to send them down south to Mississippi to work for someone else."

Olivia surprised by what John was saying looked up with a start.

"You mean he wanted to send them down south to work?"

"Yes!"

Olivia stood up walked around the table. She turned back to John.

"John you can't let them go. He's trying to trick them. First of all, it's dangerous in the south now. The KKK is killing folks left and right and The Jim Crow laws makes it hard for a Negro to live. I wouldn't go down South if you paid me $200.00. It just ain't safe. And besides that, remember I told you I had a dream about this Mr. Johnson, something just ain't right about him. You might also be in danger be careful."

John looked at his sister, listening to every word. He finished his dinner and took his plate to the sink. Then he sat back down.

"How can I warn my friends if they make up their own minds, I can't do anything to stop them."

Olivia looked at John.

"Yes! you can! Where are they now?"

"Mr. Johnson invited Robert and Max to stay and have dinner with him."

"And why do you think he did that?"

John looked at Olivia.

"To talk to them more, to change their minds."

Olivia shook her head up and down. Then she stopped and fell into the chair. She leaned her head back and closed her eyes. The room turned dark. John looked around surprised that he was witnessing one of Olivia's visions. Olivia opened her eyes they were now a bright yellow. She was looking up at the ceiling in the room. John followed her gaze and looked also. The ceiling took on the look of a screen that you would see in a movie theater.

John saw Mr. Johnson house on 19th street. As he continued to look up, he saw that it was daytime. Then he noticed a figure walking on the side of the house. It was Mr. Johnson. This was so clear and vivid its scared John. He wanted to look at Olivia, but he dared not take his eyes off of scene that was above him. Mr. Johnson continued to move toward the back of the house. John was able to see clearly the yard, porch and the alley. John gasped when he saw his friends, Robert and Max. They were standing around as if they were waiting on something.

All of a sudden, a wagon pulled up in the alley by the gate. He recognized the Coal Wagon that came to deliver every week, and wondered what it was doing there. Mr. Johnson approached the Coal Man, and they talked. Then he turned to Robert and Max. It looked like he was trying to convince them to go with the man with the Coal Wagon, but they stood back reluctant. Then John watched as Mr. Johnson and the Coal man grabbed Robert and Max forcing them to get in the wagon.

The boys struggled and fought. Then Mr. Johnson picked up a heavy branch. First, he hit Robert in the head knocking him out. Max saw this and started to run. The other man chased him and caught him knocking him down to the ground. Mr. Johnson went over to Max and knocked him in the head. The two men stood back. Then they picked up Max by his arms and legs and put him in the wagon. Next they went to Robert who was still lying on the ground, they picked him up and placed also in the wagon. Mr. Johnson took some money out of his pocket and paid the Coal Man. He then got into his wagon and drove off.

John stood in the kitchen not able to talk. Olivia still sat in the chair. He looked over at her. She now slumped and fell to the floor and appeared to be in a deep sleep. John quickly went over to his sister. He tried to wake her, but she didn't open her eyes. He picked her up and carefully carried her upstairs. He placed her in the bed and stood there looking at her. John couldn't explain what he'd saw downstairs, but something told him the scene was real. The question he asked himself was it something that had happened or was it something that was going to happen. He hoped it was the latter. He couldn't go out tonight, it would be too dangerous. But he could go back to the house very early in the morning. And stop what he'd witnessed.

CHAPTER 29

TOM JOHNSON'S PLAN

O livia woke up the next morning feeling confused. The last she remembers was having dinner with John Jr. last night, but everything else was a blur. She sat up in bed, a strong sense of dread engulfed her body. She closed her eyes, suddenly feeling dizzy. She then heard the voice of her mother May-Lynn.

"OLIVIA! JOHN JR. IS IN DANGER, "SAVE HIM."

"OLIVIA! JOHN JR. IS IN DANGER, "SAVE HIM."

"OLIVIA! JOHN JR. IS IN DANGER, "SAVE HIM."

Olivia heard her mother say this, three times. It was like a loud ringing in her ears. She placed her hands over ears trying to block out the sound, but it didn't work. She stumbled out of bed and hurried to John's room she saw his unmade bed, which meant he hadn't went to bed. Olivia now was starting to panic where was her brother.

John Jr. had gotten up early to go to Mr. Johnson's house. First, he went over to the lot looking for Robert and Max. He saw Franklin standing by the metal trash can getting ready to start a fire to stay warm. He approached him and asked.

"Hey man have you seen Robert and Max this morning?"

"No! I came here looking for them.
Didn't they go with you yesterday?"

"Yeah! I took them to work with me.
But they did come back last night, didn't they?"

Franklin looked at John Jr. in confusion.

"They went to work with me yesterday morning. Mr. Johnson met us and started asking them if they wanted to go down to Mississippi to work. I spoke against it telling the boys it wasn't a good thing to do. Well Mr. Johnson didn't agree with what I said but he did drop the subject. Then so Robert and Max wouldn't have waisted their time he allowed them to work with me. He paid them real good."

"Well! What happened to them. You left them there?"
Franklin asked.

John looked down at his feet now feeling afraid.

"Mr. Johnson offered them something to eat.

I said no thank you. They stayed I guess."

Franklin looked at John now afraid for his friends.

"Man! What do you know about this Mr. Johnson

is he a good guy?"

"I've worked for him a few months now.

He seems ok, but you never know about these white folks."

"Are you going over there now? I'm going with you."

John already heading out of the lot.

"Yeah! Let's go."

John and Franklin hurried down the street. They walked in silence. John dare not tell Franklin about the vision he saw in the kitchen last night. He wouldn't understand and would think he was crazy. John was scared for his friends, why didn't he encourage them to come back with him. He hoped nothing had happened to them.

They arrived at the House on 19th street. John headed straight to the back of the house. Before he opened the gate, he heard voices and laughter. When he entered the back yard he saw, Robert, Max and Mr. Johnson. Robert and Max were completing some of the work they'd started the day before. Franklin went over to his friends.

"Hey where you guys been all night?"

"Been right here with Tom, after we ate, it was too late to walk these streets, so we stayed in the basement. Tom took good care of us. He's alright."

John hadn't said a word but suspiciously looked at Mr. Johnson who was smiling. Then Mr. Johnson walked over to Franklin and introduced himself.

"Hey young man, you a friend of John Jr.'s?"

He reached out to shake Franklin's hand. Franklin reluctantly shook his hand and said,
"Yes!"

"Well it's good to meet you. I was just telling your friends about a great opportunity to make a lot of money. They said that they might be interested. I can let you in on it too if you're interested."

Franklin looked at Mr. Johnson.

"I might be interested, and I might not. I need to hear the details."

"I can do that, but right now are you interested in making some money today."

Franklin looked over at John Jr. who nodded that it was ok.

"Yes! I need some cash. What do I have to do?"

Mr. Johnson pointed over to John Jr.

"He'll fill you in. I'll see you men at the end of the day to pay you!"

Then he went into the house.

John looked at his friends and called them together. Then he asked Robert and Max.

"What happened last night?"

"Just like we told you. Tom fed us and it was too late to walk these streets, so we slept in the basement. John I'll tell you it was the first time in a long time I slept like a baby. You know I'm on these streets."

Max answered.

Robert shook his head in agreement. John looked at all of his friends.

"I Just want you guys to be careful. Just be careful."

He turned.

"Let's get to work."

The friends worked hard the rest of the day. They only stopped when the Negro maid brought them out sandwiches and soda. Then they finished up the day, placing the tools back in the shed. John went behind the shed to look for some chopped wood to put on the porch. He saw the wood piled up by a gate. There was a mound of dirt he had to climb over in order to get the wood. When he stepped on dirt, he felt the ground tremble. He stopped and stood still. Thinking it was his imagination he took another step. And this time the ground shook violently, throwing John to the ground. John sat there trying to figure out what had happened.

He placed his hand on the mound of dirt and was surprised that it was warm. How could this dirt be warm in the middle of Chicago's autumn weather? John got up leaving the woods and went back to his friends. Mr. Johnson came out and paid the young men. He was very satisfied with the work and complemented them. It was getting late and John suggested that they head home. He and Franklin headed toward the gate. When they looked back, they saw that Robert and Max were not following. John stopped.

"Hey guys are you coming?"
Robert and Max looked at John and Franklin, Max spoke.

"Man Mr. Johnson said as long as we worked for him, he'll give us a place to stay. And you know me, and Robert don't have no place to stay. And it's getting cold in these streets. So, we gonna take advantage of this for a little while at least."

Franklin looked at John. And stepped to him.
"I'll stay here with them and watch out.
He can't do nothing to all of us."

John looked at Franklin and nodded his head.
"Ok! I'll see you guys in the morning."

John reluctantly left his friends at the house. But Franklin was right, Mr. Johnson, couldn't attack all of them at the same time, and he trusted that his friends would handle the situation. John walked home thinking about everything that had happened in the last few days. The fact is that he didn't trust Mr. Johnson and he was definitely up to something. John reached the house and saw that Olivia was up. He sat down at the kitchen table. Olivia looked at her brother, with concern on her face.

"I went looking for you this morning,

but I discovered you had left. Is everything Ok?"

John looked at Olivia and answered.

"Not really but I don't know what to think of everything that's been happening. Mr. Johnson has taken a personal interest in my friends. He's trying to recruit them to work down in Mississippi, but I feel that he's setting up a trap for them. If they went down there, I may never see them again."

Olivia sat listening closely to John Jr.

"John what happened last night?"

John looked at her in surprise.

"You don't remember, do you?"

"All I remember is that I was sitting at this table eating dinner, we were talking and when I woke up it was the next morning and I was in my bed."

John stood up and walked around the table. He stood and faced Olivia.

"I guess you showed me a vision. And that has never happened before. And I can't explain why because I've always been in the dark about your visions. But last night you let me see, what might or is going to happen."

"Can you tell me what you saw?"
John sat down.

"Olivia! I don't know if it's something I can tell, you were here when it was happening, do you remember anything?"

"No! I don't. That's why I'm asking you. You have to tell me what happened so I can help you." Olivia said angrily.

"But you don't know if you can help me. Maybe you weren't allowed to see the vision because it was meant only for me. And that's what the spirit is telling me. This is something I have to fix, and I intend on fixing it. So don't worry about me."

John exited the kitchen and went to his room. Olivia yelled after him, but he didn't come back. Olivia continued to sit there for once not knowing what to do. Maybe John was right. She wasn't given any insight on what was happening or what was going to happen. Suddenly the kitchen became dark, and there was a yellow glow above Olivia's head.

She looked up at the ceiling and saw a vision of her mother. May-Lynn smiled at her daughter.

"Hello my child. Your brother is right, this is not your battle. Let him do what he has to do."

"But mother you called to me this morning that I had to save John Jr. You told me that this morning."

"Yes! I remember saying that to you. But daughter there are lots of ways someone can be saved."

"Mama is John Jr. going to get killed just like daddy?"

May-Lynn's face started fading.

"Mama! Mama! Don't go."

May-Lynn spoke:

"You'll see. In time everything will be revealed to you and that's how you'll save John Jr."

THIRTY

THE KILLING

John Jr. had trouble sleeping that night. He kept waking up seeing his friends being taken away in the Coal Wagon. Today he was determined to stop it all. He was going to get his friends from Mr. Johnson's house. The man was very dangerous. John got up and put on his clothes. He stopped at Olivia's room, but she was fast asleep. He started exit the house, then he went back to the kitchen. He took one of Ma Ellen's meat knives and put it in his pocket. Then he went on the porch and down the steps. He walked quickly toward the house on 19th street. As he got closer, he quickened his steps. He felt doom as he approached the house. John started running. He went down the side of the house and opened the gate to the backyard. There he saw two men carrying Max, who looked like a limp rag into a wagon.

John yelled:

"STOP!"

The men looked around and hurried in what they were doing.

John yelled again:

"STOP I SAID! I'M GOING FOR THE POLICE!"

The men suddenly dropped Max on the ground, they ran to the wagon and took off. John rushed over to Max who was lying still and not moving. He reached down to check his friend he saw that he was still breathing. All of a sudden Robert and Franklin stumbled out of the basement. They reached John and Max. Robert hardly speaking audible, said:

"That white cracker drugged us. We was, drinking last night and when we tried to get up this morning we couldn't walk."

John looked at his friends,
"Can you walk now?"

They shook their heads yes.
"Help me pick up Max and let's get out of here."

John looked around but he didn't see Tom Johnson. Max was starting to come too. He mumbled:
"Where am I?"

"Don't worry man we got ya!"

John glanced around he didn't see Mr. Johnson. He just knew he would come back and deal with him later. The boys hurried out of the back yard, holding Max. They took a short cut through the park. And walked down Ogden Blvd. When they got back to the lot, they stopped to rest. If anybody was chasing them, they knew better than to venture into their neighborhood. Someone found some water and gave it to Max to drink, he looked up at his friends.

"John thank you. You came just in time. Those gangsters came into that basement and dragged me out of bed. I started fighting but I ain't had no strength. Before I knew it, I was being carried outside to that wagon."

John said;
"Mr. Johnson was too anxious about talking you guys into going down south. Those white folks down there are lynching Niggers when they get off the train. Well it's over now. Stay away from Tom Johnson."

The guys nodded their heads in agreement. Robert spoke.
"Yeah! About that Tom Johnson we should go back over there and kick his behind."

John spoke:

"Don't ya'll worry about him he's gonna get his. I'll make sure of that."

Franklin invited Robert and Max to stay with him. He lived with his oldest brother and if the boys were willing to work for him, he's sure he would allow them to live with him. They all said good night and walked out of the lot. John turned toward his house, but when he his friends could no longer see he headed toward the house on 19th street.John went back to North Lawndale and sat by a tree in the park.

It was starting to get dark and he could see many colored workers heading back to their neighborhoods. John stayed out of sight especially when the Police started cruising the area. John stationed himself on a hill in Douglas Park. From this spot he could see Tom Johnson's house. He saw when the maid left, and that meant that Mr. Johnson was in the house alone with his wife. He still had the knife in his pocket. John waited, he sat on that hill waiting for the right time to confront. Tom Johnson.

About 9:00 p.m. John looked over at the house. The light in the front, was no longer on so maybe that meant that they'd gone to bed. He slowly got up and walked down the hill toward the house. He crossed the street and went up on the porch. John looked in the window, it was dark, and he couldn't see any movement.

He lightly tapped on the window and waited.

He tapped again, a little louder. Still no movement.

He tapped one more time. This time a light upstairs came on. John moved away from the door. He heard movement in the hall, and someone was turning the lock. Tom Johnson slowly opened the door and looked out on the porch. He jumped when John suddenly appeared in front, of him. He looked at John afraid.

"What! Are you doing here?"

"I Came to give you a message."

"What message?"

"You don't mess with me and mine. I knew what you was up all along. Tom Johnson slavery is dead! And it ain't coming back. So, if you think you gonna recruit some colors back down south to work for you for free. You are barking up the wrong tree. And to make sure it don't happen, I'm gonna warn every color person I know to stay away from Tom Johnson."

"Why you uppity Nigger. Who do you think your talking too?"

Mr. Johnson lunged at John. John pulled out the knife and swung it at Tom. Tom jumped back and missing the knife. John came at him again. Tom grabbed John around his neck choking him. John pulled at his hands trying to loosen Tom's grip. But Tom held fast. John started losing consciousness, and soon he fell on the porch. Tom kneeled down next to John, he felt for a pulse and didn't get one. Tom glanced up and down the dark street looking to see if anyone witnessed what had just happened. He also looked next door to his neighbors and didn't see any lights. Tom dragged John down the stairs, bumping his head hard on each step. Then he proceeded to pulled John by his feet and took him to the back yard.

He opened the gate and pulled John through the debris to the back of the shed. He went inside and brought out a shovel. He remembered the last time he had dug a grave back here. And now he had to dig another one. He immediately started digging in the same spot where he had buried Paul. When he had dug deep enough, a dim light came from the sky and fell on the grave. The light shone directly on Paul's bones. But what was so strange was that Paul's head was completely whole. The rest of his body was only bones, but the head and face were still in tack. Tom froze, holding the shovel in the air. Tom bent down and looked closer, he saw Paul's face his eyes were wide open, and he was looking directly at him. Tom dropped the shovel and backed up in the yard. He stumbled over John Jr. He stood there trying to compose himself.

"Ok! Get it together, you got to bury this Nigger."

Tom shook off his fear and grabbed John Jr's feet he dragged him to the open grave and dumped him on top of Paul. Then he quickly started covering up the body. All the time he was putting dirt on top of John and Paul, the light from the sky kept shining on the grave. At one time while covering the bodies. Tom swore he could hear voices. A woman, screaming, a man yelling. He hurriedly covered the body's and went back into the house. He entered the bedroom shaking. His wife sat up and looked at him.

"Tom! Where were you?"

Tom stuttered:
"I heard a noise and went outside to check on things."

His wife laid back down.

"Did you see anything?'

"No! it wasn't nothing! Go back to sleep."

Tom laid there the rest of the night terrified about what he'd done. Where did that light come from? And Paul's head laying there with those penetrating eyes. Was he being punished? The next morning Olivia woke up with a start. John! Where was he? She jumped out of bed and ran to his room. The door was closed, was he still asleep? Slowly opening the door Olivia was hit with a cold blast, the room was freezing. Olivia went over to the bed but didn't see John.

She looked around noticing that walls were completely covered with ice. Ice cycles hung from the dresser, lamp and table. A thin layer of ice covered the bed quilt. Olivia went over to the lamp and broke off an ice cycle, it burned her hand. She dropped it and it crashed on the floor. Olivia continued to look at the room, she'd never seen anything like this before and she didn't know what to make of it. But what was more important John was missing and she needed to find him.

She left the room and went back to her room to get dressed. She'd find his friends and check his hangouts. Surely there was someone who had seen John yesterday. Olivia quietly got dressed and left the house. She was careful not to wake Jacob and Ma Ellen. She started walking toward a lot where she'd seen some of John's friends. As she walked along, she started thinking about all of the warning signs that had been shown to her. Signs from her mother, Ma Ellen, even her father. She remembers the morning when she heard her mother's voice.

"JOHN JR. IS IN DANGER! SAVE HIM!"

But her mother forgot to tell how to save him. Olivia felt deep in her soul that John was dead, and if he was, she didn't do anything to save him. But what could she do? She approached the lot and saw three men standing around a lit garbage can trying to stay warm. When she closer she was able to recognize Robert, Max and Franklin. They looked up in surprise when they saw her. Franklin spoke up.

"Hey! Your John's sister, right?
What's your name again?
Olivia, Olivia that's your name."

Then he looked at his friends and they all smiled.
"What can we do for you? And Where's John."

"I came to ask you the same thing.
He didn't come home last night."

The guys looked at each other. Max said,
"What do you mean he didn't home last night?"

"He didn't come home, have you seen him?"

The men looked down at their feet and Robert stirred the fire with a stick. Franklin spoke and addressed his friends.

"We need to come clean with Olivia."

Franklin told Olivia the whole story of how Mr. Johnson was trying to get them to go down south to work on a farm. And how John was warning them about Mr. Johnson. He also told Olivia how the night before Mr. Johnson had drugged them, and the next morning some men came to load them into wagons, before John came and stopped them. Olivia listened getting more and more afraid for John.

"Well what happened to John?"

The guys looked at each other. Max answered.
"He must have went back to confront Mr. Johnson."

Olivia walked around in a panic.
"He hasn't been home all night.
Where does this Mr. Johnson live?"

Franklin went over to Olivia and faced her.

"You don't plan on going over there do you? That wouldn't be good. Hey, let us go and find out what happened to John and we'll get back to you."

Olivia looked at Franklin and glanced back at the other guys. He was right she couldn't do anything, so she would have to trust them to find John.

"Ok! Please find John and get back to me as soon as possible. I'd really appreciate it."

Olivia turned to leave. She had to go back to the house and tell Jacob and Ma Ellen what was going on. When Olivia left the boys looked at each other. Robert spoke first.

"You guys know what happened. John went back over there last night to confront Tom Johnson. Something bad must have happened. We got to go back and look for John. He saved us, now we got to save him. lets' go guys."

The guys set to see a Tom Johnson in North Lawndale.

THIRTY-ONE

REVENGING JOHN JR'S DEATH

Olivia went back to the house. Ma Ellen met her at the door.

"John Jr. is missing!"

Olivia came into the house and sat at the kitchen table. She faced Ma Ellen.

"I just saw John's friends and they told me that the man John worked for was trying to recruit young Negros back to Mississippi to work on farms. John went to the house just in time to stop some men who was putting his friends in a wagon. Ma Ellen I don't know what to do."

Ma Ellen looked at Olivia and touch her hand.

"I'm so sorry sweetie but the African Spirits are in charge now, and there's nothing we can do. It's out of our hands."

"Ma Ellen! I can't accept that. This is my brother and if he's in danger I need to help. I'm gonna call the police."

Olivia went to pick up the phone. But Ma Ellen's voice stopped her.

"Girl you know the police ain't gonna get involved in this. They don't care about Negro's going missin. In fact, the more missin the better."

Ma Ellen left the room. Olivia continued to sit. Wondering how she could help John. Jacob came into the room and sat down next to Olivia.

"Ma Ellen told me that John Jr. is missin. What happened?

Olivia repeated the story to Jacob.

"All I know is that John's friends are on their way over to Mr. Johnson's house right now. To find John. But something tells me that things are only going to get worse."

Max, Robert and Franklin started walking toward Mr. Johnson's house. They were silent as they hurried to the house on 19th street. They cut through the park and stopped on top of the hill. The group stood there, looking at the house. Franklin was the first to speak up.

"Well what do you think?"

Max answered:
"What do you mean? We're going over there and we're going to talk to Mr. Johnson. We're going to ask him if he's seen John."

Robert spoke next.
"And what if he says, he ain't seen him."

Franklin said:
"Then we do some investigating, because I don't trust anything coming out of that man's mouth."

"OK! let's go."
Said Max.

The group went down the hill and across the street to the house. They walked up on the porch and knocked on the door. It took a few minutes, but soon the maid came to the door. She looked at the young men and asked.

"What ya'll doing here?"

Max answered.

"Remember us? We're John Jr. friends.
We was here a few days ago working."

"I remember ya. I heard you was fired,
so why are you here now?"

The guys looked at each other. Then back at the maid. Robert stepped up towering over her.

"Listen girl. Our friend John is missin, and the last place we saw him was here. We need to speak to Mr. Johnson."

The maid suddenly looked scared. She anxiously looked behind her and stepped out on the porch. She motioned the boys to come closer. The look on her face told them that she knew something. She started speaking in a scared whisper.

"Mr. Johnson ain't here. But last night, I stayed here because it was too late to go home. I was sleep when I heard some voices out here on the porch. It was Mr. Johnson and the other man sounded like John. They were yelling at each other. Then I heard a lot of rumbling like they were fighting. Then it was quiet."

The guys looked at each other. Max spoke:

"Is Mr. Johnson around?"

The maid answered:

"Naw! He went out early this morning. But he wasn't in a good mood. Going around the house yelling at everybody."

The boys turned and left.

The guys left the porch and stood on the sidewalk. They didn't say anything. They looked back at the door and noticed that the maid had gone back in the house. Then Franklin motioned for the guys to follow him. They walked to the side of the house and walked down the path that led to the backyard. They quietly opened the gate and walked into the yard.

They started looking around for their friend. They searched under the porch, and looked in the windows of the basement, and opened the shed, but didn't see anything. Franklin ventured behind the shed, looking behind the wood pile, but no John. Then he noticed the loose dirt, under his feet. He bent down and was able to pick up a handful, which meant that someone had been digging in the ground. He stood and called his friends. Max and Robert came and stood beside him.

"Did you find something?"

"This is fresh dirt. Which means somebody's
been digging in this spot."

Robert looked around for something to dig with. Max fell to his knees and started removing dirt with his hands. Franklin fell down beside him and started grabbing dirt and tossing it aside. The boys frantically tossed handfuls of dirt trying to see what was buried beneath. Suddenly the sound of a voice was heard above them.

"What are you boys doing here?"

Max and Robert stood up at the sound of Tom Johnson's voice. But Franklin kept digging, now grabbing a stick and to remove the dirt.

"We came back to look for our boy John.
He didn't come home last night."

Mr. Johnson looked at Robert.

"What that got to do with me. Now you boys need to get off my
property. I ain't seen John Jr. And we ain't got no business since
you boys ain't gonna work for me. Now I need you Niggers to leave
my property right now."

Franklin who was still digging stood up and pointed to the ground.

"What's under here? What's buried under that dirt?"

Mr. Johnson moved and stepped in front of Franklin to block him from digging.

"Ain't nothing under that dirt. You ain't got no rights here, you boys need to leave."

He then pushed Franklin causing him to fall down. Max and Robert took up the cause and attacked Tom Johnson. They beat him down to the ground. Punching and kicking him. Franklin regaining his stance stood he pick up a brick that was lying near the shed, he picked it up and bashed Tom Johnson in the head. The boys stood up looking down at Tom, who wasn't moving. Lying there with a big gash in his head he didn't move. Max whispered in horror.

"Man! He's dead!'

Franklin looked at the brick in his hand and dropped it.
"I just know he did something to John Jr. I just know it!"

Robert looked around in panic:
"We can't do nothin about that now!

We gotta get out of here, now."

Robert and Max took off running.

Franklin paused looking down at the spot where he had been digging. He stumbled over Tom Johnson and quickly ran catching up with the others. The boys ran and ran leaving the neighborhood, where they'd just committed a crime. They ran through the park, between the trees, jumping over bushes. Franklin found himself looking over his shoulder to see if anyone was following them.

They slowed down when they reached Western Blvd. Standing on the corner, they decided to walk the rest of the way not cause alarm from people on the street. They continued to walk till they reached the lot. They sat there for a long time not saying a word. Max spoke.

"We just killed a man!"

Franklin responded:

"He deserved it. That man killed John Jr. I just know he did. I believe John is buried behind that shed. He went back to see Mr. Johnson last night, they got into an argument and he killed him."

Robert asked:

"But why would he kill John?"

"John was gonna rat him out about sending Niggers back down South to work like slaves. John knew all about it and he was gonna tell."

"Well we'll never know, cause we ain't never going back to that house."

In the coming days the boys would look in the Sun Times and The Tribune to see if there was any news about a murder, but nothing ever appeared. Back at the house Olivia was waiting for John's friends to see her. But when they didn't come back that same day with no news, she assumed that everything was ok, and maybe they were all hanging out somewhere in the neighborhood. But she would get on her brother for not checking in with her, Jacob and Ma Ellen to let them know he was safe.

It was early Saturday morning the third day, and the guys decided that it was time for them to see Olivia. They were still hoping in the back of their minds that John Jr. would miraculously appear, but that hadn't happened. They met at the lot and then set off to the house where Olivia was staying with Jacob and Ma Ellen. When they reached the house, they stood outside the gate. Looking at the front door. None of them wanted to do this. They all had grown to like John Jr.'s sister, and she didn't deserve this, but she needed to be told.

They walked up the path and stood on the porch. Franklin knocked on the door. Someone yelled from the other side.

"Just a minute!"

Then Ma Ellen, opened the door. She looked at the boys and smiled, then her expression changed. She started backing up into the living room, calling for Olivia to come downstairs. The boys stepped into the house. They cautiously looked at each other not daring to speak. Olivia slowly came down the stairs. She looked at Max, Robert and Franklin.

"You didn't find him did ya?"

The boys slowly shook their heads. Olivia sat down on the couch and started rocking. Ma Ellen was on the other side of the room with her eyes closed. Talking in an unknown language. Olivia motioned for the boys to sit down.

"We'd rather stand if you don't mind. We ain't gonna stay long."
Max spoke.

Then each of them taking turns started telling Olivia about their visit to see Mr. Johnson, what the maid had told them, and about them searching the back of the house, looking for John Jr. After they'd finished Olivia asked them.

"So, you didn't find him?"

They shook their heads, affirming what they'd said.

"So, did you see Mr. Johnson?"

The guys looked at each other and started moving around nervously. Max spoke rushing his words.

"You see Mr. Johnson caught us when we were in the back. He asked what we were doing, and we questioned him about John, he lied and said that he hadn't seen him then he pushed Franklin then we jumped on him. We hit him in the head with a brick, and he fell down, dead."

Olivia looked at the boys with shock and disbelief on her face. She slowly got up from the couch and went over to the window. She looked out at the people who started to gather on the street, then she turned back to the boys.

"You didn't kill Mr. Johnson!"

The guys gasped and all started talking at one time.

"What do you mean, we didn't kill him we saw him lying on the ground with his head bashed in."

"Oh! Yes I saw him with his head bandaged up, and when I asked him about it, he said that he had fell. But he came by the house yesterday because he was concerned. He'd heard that John Jr. was missing, and he wanted to know if he been found."

Franklin stepped over to Olivia.

"What did you tell him?"

"I told him that John hadn't been home for a few days and that all of us was out looking for him. Then he looked at me strange and told me that he and John had spoken, and they'd settled their disagreement. He told me that John wanted to more into going to work in Mississippi. And he was thinking that he just might take a trip down there to check it out."

The boys looked at each other in disbelief. Franklin walked around the room angrily moving his arms and shaking his head.

"He's lying, Olivia He lied to you. John would never leave here like that without telling somebody where he was going."

Olivia looked at Franklin and shook her head.

"*I know Mr. Johnson is hiding something, and he want us to believe that John Jr. left town. I know my brother and it just ain't so. But how can I prove him wrong?*"

I know said Max.

"*We go back over there and finish digging behind that shed.*"

Olivia looked at Max.
"*What shed and digging for what?*"

The guys looked at each other.
"*We believe that Mr. Johnson killed John and buried him in his back yard behind his shed. That's we were doing when he caught us.*"

"*No! you can't go back over there if it was dangerous for John Jr. You know you'll be in dangerous for you guys too. Stay from over there. I'm gonna call the police and report this information!*" Olivia yelled.

"*Ain't no Chicago Police caring about no Nigger. They'll pretend they looking for him but you know they ain't looking for nobody,*" Robert said.

*"Well it's no longer in your hands. I thank you boys. But as of this day and time. **Leave it alone.**"*

Olivia turned and went upstairs. The boys turned and left the house. Collectively they knew what they had to do, they were going back over to the house and dig behind that shed. But it would be tonight. The boys decided to meet in Douglas Park. They knew it wouldn't be good to walk over to the house together because of police patrolling the area. Max got to the park first. He sat on the hill in the park away from the streetlights but just enough light for him to see the house. The drapes on the window's hadn't been closed so he was able to see movement in the house. Mr. Johnson and his wife were sitting down and having their dinner. Max felt a hand on his shoulder and almost jumped out of his skin, it was Robert.

"Man! Why did you sneak up on me like that?
I could've knocked you out."
Robert was laughing at his friend.

"Man, you too scary. Franklin not here yet."

Max put his finger to his lips.
"Stop being so loud. Ain't nobody around
but that don't mean nobody's listening."

Robert looked at his friend.

Laughing, he asked,
"Man! What does that mean?"

"It means be quiet!"

Robert shook his head and sat down beside Max.
"What's happening?"

"Nothing much. I just see Johnson and his wife walking around talking. They had dinner earlier, so hopefully they are getting ready for bed."

"Have you seen that maid around?"

"I saw her leave before it got dark.
So! they the only ones in the house."

They continued to sit and turned when they heard someone approaching. It was Franklin. He crawled up beside his friends, asking a question only with his eyes. All of them stood.

"Let's do this!"

By this time the lights in the house were off. The boys quietly crossed the street to the house. Careful not to step on any dried leaves or branches, they walked down the path that led to the back of the house. Slowly opening the gate, they were glad for the small lantern that lit up the ally. But Franklin had thought ahead and brought matches and a candle, that he hoped he wouldn't have to use. They walked to the back of the yard, behind the shed. Max took a step and suddenly fell. When he looked around him, he noticed a big hole.

Franklin took out his matches and the candle. He struck the match and lit the candle holding it over where Max had fallen. The light shined on a large hole. But what was in the hole made the boys shake. As Franklin held the light closer. He gasped when he saw John Jr. body. His was face up and the boys could see that he was starting to decay. His jaws were slack, and his skin was wrinkled and showing his bones. Franklin dropped the candle. The guys looked at each other in the dark. What were they going to do?

All of a sudden there was a noise behind them. Three men ran up on the boys and took them down. They clubbed them with sticks and bricks. Mr. Johnson stood quietly on the side watching. When the fight was over. Max, Robert and Franklin were lying on the ground. Franklin was barely conscious. He laid there not daring to move fearing that he would be hit again. He looked over to see if he could see his friends, Max was laying on his side moaning and Robert was on his back with his eyes closed. Then he heard one of the men speak to Mr. Johnson.

"One's dead but the other two barely alive.

What you want us to do with them?"

Mr. Johnson came and stood over the boys, with his arms folded across his chest. His voice was cold.

"Take them Niggers to the woods and shoot them in the head. That's what we'd do in Mississippi. But a Nigger is a Nigger whether in Chicago or Mississippi. Get rid of them."

Mr. Johnson took a wad of cash from his pocket and paid the men.

"What about that one in the hole?"

"No, leave him, he's already decaying. Leave him here."

Then Tom Johnson walked back to his house. Franklin knew that he and his friend's fate was near. He started to get up he wasn't going to die without a fight. He raised up and one of the men saw him. Franklin yelled out but the other man came behind him and clubbed in the head with a brick. Franklin fell back on the ground; Unconsciousness took over his body.

The men gathered the three boys and dumped in a wagon, and silently drove away.

THIRTY-TWO

WHERE'S MY BROTHER

The meeting with John's friends had greatly disturbed Olivia. She was shocked when they told her they'd attacked Mr. Johnson, what were they thinking? She was glad for their sake that he hadn't died. But the question still lingered in the air, where was John Jr.? The boys had mentioned looking in Mr. Johnson's backyard digging behind a shed. What was buried behind the shed? Should she try to find out herself or leave everything to the police?

Olivia woke up the next morning determined to go to the police station. She would report that John was missing and see what the authorities would do. She went downstairs and found Ma Ellen fixing breakfast.

"Good morning Ma Ellen!"

Ma Ellen didn't answer. In fact, she didn't even turn around to look at Olivia. Then she spoke in a low voice. *"Olivia, don't go to the Police."*

Olivia looked at Ma Ellen.

"Ma Ellen did you say something?'

Ma Ellen turned and faced Olivia.

"I said don't go to the Police.

They ain't gonna help you."

Olivia sat down at the table.

"You know something about John Jr, don't you?'

Ma Ellen sat across from Olivia. There were tears in her eyes.

"This is bigger than anything the Police can help you with. There are five Negro Boys dead. And they died at the hands of a white man. Now when you tell the police that, what do you think they gonna do?"

Ma Ellen stood and went back to cooking breakfast. Olivia looked at Ma Ellen's back hoping she would say more. Suddenly a cold wind swept through the kitchen. It was so cold Olivia started shivering. It got so dark Olivia could no longer see Ma Ellen. A light from above shown in the room. Olivia looked up and was able to see the sky. As she looked closer, she saw a total of five clouds.

She stood from her chair. As she looked closer, she saw the clouds start to form facial features, she gasped when she recognized, Max,

Robert, Franklin and John Jr. she placed her hand over her mouth not wanting to scream. Olivia continued to look, she noticed that the fifth cloud was still forming, it was a face she didn't recognize.

The following weeks Olivia stayed close to the house. She followed Ma Ellen's advice and didn't go to the Police. But she did place an ad in the Chicago Defender asking if anyone had seen John Jr. The Chicago Defender was a newspaper published by Negros for Negros.

One day while looking through the Defender, Olivia saw the haunting faces of John Jr.'s friends. Staring back at her on the entire page was pictures of Max, Robert and Franklin.

The headline read:

HAVE YOU SEEN THESE BOYS?
MAX THOMPSON
ROBERT JONES
FRANKLIN HOLLIS

There was also a picture of another young man that reminded Olivia of someone she'd seen before, but she couldn't remember where. She took the paper in the house to read the article. It said that the boys had been missing for about a week. And that they were last seen in the North Lawndale area. The other young man was named *Paul Jackson*. He hadn't been seen in two months, and like the other boys Paul also was last seen in the North Lawndale area. Olivia sat straight up now she realized that this was the same boy who face was shown in the clouds, with the other four. Had all of these boys been killed? And had they been killed by the same person in the North Lawndale neighborhood?

Six months later there still was no sign of John Jr. Someone discovered some human bones in a forest preserve on the outside of town. It was never discovered who they belonged to. Olivia visited the house on 19th street looking for Mr. Johnson, the neighbors said that he and his wife had moved back to Mississippi. The house was now owned by another family. Olivia decided not to bother them.

Ten Years Later

Olivia had finished high school and took a job in a downtown office. She continued to live with Jacob and Ma Ellen, who were now getting older and needed her to take care of them. In 1949 Ma Ellen got sick with cancer and passed away. Jacob was heartbroken. He wandered around the house for months, not caring whether he lived or died. Olivia tried her best to comfort him, but nothing worked. One day he left the house and didn't come back. Olivia was immediately concerned and went out looking for him. After walking the streets and checking with Jacobs friends, she still couldn't find him. After a week had passed, she decided to check the city morgue. Olivia was told that Jacob had been hit by a car, and he died at the scene. He didn't have any identification; therefore no one was notified. Olivia was now alone.

Jacob and Ma Ellen had left the house to Olivia to which she was very grateful. Olivia continued to live in the only house she knew since coming to Chicago. Sometimes at night she would hear the spirits of her family. They would gather at night while she slept. They watched over her and kept her safe. Olivia got old and at the age of 60 she had retired from working. She would get up in the morning and make herself some breakfast. She would always set the table for herself and one other person. She would sit there and talk to her mother, sometimes to her father and of course Jacob and Ma Ellen.

She never talked to John Jr. And this disturbed her greatly. One night after going to bed. Olivia started to dream. She remembers standing in the park watching the house on 19th street. As she stood there a little Negro girl came out and stood on the porch. She looked right at Olivia and raised her hand and waved. Olivia slowly raised her hand and waved back.

Olivia sat straight up in bed. Then she spoke to herself.

IN THE YEAR 1963, A LITTLE GIRL BY THE NAME OF OPHELIA WILL HELP ME DISCOVER WHAT HAPPENED TO MY BROTHER, JOHN JR.

THE END

www.ingramcontent.com/pod-product-compliance
Lightning Source LLC
Chambersburg PA
CBHW051131020726
47501CB00005B/1449